"I Want You."

"I realize that," Olivia said cautiously. "There's just one problem."

"And what would that be?"

"Your relationship with my father."

Mac's brows lifted just slightly, then he scowled.

"He called this morning and said you might be stopping by."

"Did he?"

"Yep." She looked him straight in the eye. "Now, Mr. Valentine, why don't you tell me why you're really here?"

Dear Reader,

What would you do if someone set out to ruin your reputation? Take down your business? Destroy everything you've worked so hard to achieve? *Is your blood boiling yet?*

These are the questions I wanted to have my hero, Mac Valentine, face in book two of the NO RING REQUIRED series. I wanted to see how far he would go, how ruthless he would be in destroying the man who was so out to destroy him.

Honestly, I've felt Mac's anger—that roaring sound of injustice that rings in your ears every time you think about how you've been screwed over. Maybe you have, too, and you want your payback. But after you have it, is the satisfaction of making that person pay enough? Does it heal you?

Let me know what you think about Mac and Olivia's story. And, if you want to share your story, I'd love to hear it. E-mail me at laura@laurawright.com.

All my best,

Laura

LAURA WRIGHT

PLAYBOY'S RUTHLESS PAYBACK

Published by Silhouette Books

America's Publisher of Contemporary Romance

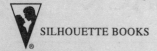

SILHOUETTE BOOKS

ISBN-13: 978-0-373-76834-9
ISBN-10:   0-373-76834-6

PLAYBOY'S RUTHLESS PAYBACK

Recent books by Laura Wright

Silhouette Desire

Locked up with a Lawman #1553
Redwolf's Woman #1582
A Bed of Sand #1607
The Sultan's Bed #1661
Her Royal Bed #1674
Savor the Seduction #1687
Millionaire's Calculated Baby Bid #1828
Playboy's Ruthless Payback #1834

*No Ring Required

LAURA WRIGHT

has spent most of her life immersed in the world of acting, singing and competitive ballroom dancing. But when she started writing romance, she knew she'd found her true calling! Born and raised in Minneapolis, Laura has also lived in New York, Ohio and Wisconsin. Currently, she has set down her bags in Los Angeles, California, and although the town can be a little crazy at times, Laura is grateful to have her theatrical production manager husband, two young children and three dogs to keep her sane. During her downtime, Laura loves to paint, play peek-a-boo with her little boy, go to movies with her husband and read with her daughter. She loves hearing from her readers and can be reached at P.O. Box 57523 Sherman Oaks, CA 91413.

To Daniel, thank you for seeing me through this book.
You're the best!

One

"Congresswoman Fisher is on line two, Derek Mead is still holding on line three and Owen Winston is on line four."

Mac Valentine relaxed in his chair. His executive assistant, Claire, stood in the doorway of his modern, chrome-and-leather penthouse office, an expectant look on her grandmotherly face. She had been with him for eight years and she was somewhat of a voyeur when it came to watching him work. She especially enjoyed moments like this when he was about to crush someone. She thought of him as a ruthless, unflinching businessman, and on more than one occasion he'd heard her refer to him as a black-haired, black-eyed demon who held each one of his thirty-five employees to incredibly high standards.

Mac grinned. The woman was right. The only thing she'd left out was that if any one of those employees fell short of his expectations, if they didn't strive for the goal of making MCV Wealth Enhancement Corp. the first choice of not only the Minneapolis area, but also the entire Midwest, they were sent packing.

Behind her black frames, Claire's eyes glistened like a child waiting for dessert to be served. "Mr. Winston says he is returning your call, sir."

Mac palmed his BlackBerry. "Tell both the congresswoman and Mead that I'll return their calls. This won't take long."

"Yes, sir." Claire hovered in the doorway.

"And close the door when you go," Mac said evenly. "Today is not a school day."

"Of course, sir." Looking thoroughly disappointed, Claire left the room.

Mac pressed the call button and leaned back in his chair. "Owen."

"That's right," came the irritated voice on the other end of the line. "I've been holding for longer than I care to. What can I do for you?"

Satisfaction rolled through Mac at the slight tremor in the older man's voice. He turned his chair toward the wall of windows behind him and stared out at the view of the Minneapolis skyline. "I won't waste my time or yours asking why you did what you did."

"Excuse me?"

"Or force you to admit it," said Mac. "Attempting to ruin the reputation of a competing firm happens quite a bit in our game. Mostly with the older set. You guys get tired, lose your edge and the clients start looking elsewhere."

Mac could practically see Owen's face darkening with rage. "You don't know what you're talking about, Valentine—"

"You can't help it," Mac continued coldly. "You see these hotshots coming up the ranks with cooler heads and sharper minds and you start to worry that you're not going to be taken seriously anymore. And when you realize it's only a matter of time before you're forced out of business, you panic." Mac leaned forward and said without emotion, "You panicked, Owen."

"This is ridiculous," Owen sputtered. "You don't know what you're talking about."

Mac continued as if he hadn't heard. "A respectable man would recognize his limitations and retire, maybe play a round of golf in the morning followed by a nice nap in the afternoon."

"A respectable businessman, Valentine." Owen laughed bitterly. "A respectable businessman wouldn't give preferential treatment, key information or tips to certain privileged clients. A respectable man wouldn't give that information based on their client's long legs and large breasts."

It was the accusation of a desperate man, total BS, but the rumor had spread like the flu. "You are this close to a lawsuit, Winston."

"That sharp mind of yours would never allow these observations of mine to go on the record in a court of law. Such a long, drawn-out process. Even worse for your reputation, I would think."

It took a few seconds for Mac to respond, then a deadly calm crept over him like the blackening sky before a thunderstorm. "True enough," he said slowly. "Perhaps legal recourse isn't the right way to deal with you."

"Smart man. Now it's late and I have—"

Mac stood and walked across the room. "No, I suppose I'll have to come up with a different way to make you pay for what you've done."

"It's after seven, Valentine," said Owen tightly. "I have dinner plans."

"Yes, of course—get home to your family." Mac opened his office door and gestured for Claire. "Especially that lovely daughter of yours. What's her name again? Allison? Olive?"

Owen didn't answer.

"Ah, right…" Mac raised a brow at Claire. "Olivia. Beautiful name," Mac said as he watched his assistant go to her computer and begin a search. "Beautiful name for a beautiful woman, I'm told. You know, your daughter has a reputation for being a very good girl. Sweet, loves her father and steers clear of anything scandalous. Might be interesting to see how easy or how enjoyably difficult it would be to change that."

Claire glanced up, her expression a mixed bag of respect, curiosity and horror.

"You stay away from my daughter." The once cocky old man now sounded like an anxious pup.

"I'm not a religious man, Owen, but I believe the

phrase 'an eye for an eye' is appropriate here." Mac stalked back into his office. "I may be an arrogant, selfish prick, but I'm no fraud. I give every one of my clients two hundred percent, male and female alike. You went too far."

Mac stabbed at the off button on his BlackBerry and walked to the windows. The bleak, gray light of a hostile rainstorm hovered over the parking lot and street below, making Mac feel as though his threats to Owen Winston might be so powerful they could not only affect the sexual status of an innocent young woman, but the weather, as well.

"She owns No Ring Required."

Mac didn't turn around to address Claire's statement. "How do I know that name?"

"*Minneapolis Magazine* did a cover story on the business last month. Three women—a chef, an interior designer and a party planner—all top-notch business-women who have banded together to create—"

"A service for men who need the help and expertise of a wife," he continued. "But either don't have one or don't want one."

"That's right."

He turned around and nodded to his assistant. "Perfect. Set up an appointment with Olivia Winston for this week. It would seem that I'm in need of her services."

"Did you read the article, sir?"

"I don't remember…I probably skimmed it."

"These are hardcore, upstanding women who are well-respected in the business community. They are adamantly against any and all fraternization."

Mac grinned to himself. "Get that appointment for tomorrow morning. First thing."

Lip pulled under her teeth, Claire nodded and left the room.

Mac returned to his desk and thumbed through the files of the clients that had gone AWOL since Owen Winston's lies had surfaced two days ago. Who knew if they were ever going to return to his company or if their relationship with his firm was dead in the water.

Mac wanted to throttle that bastard—but violence was too quickly given and gotten over. No, it would have to be a rep for a rep. Owen had taken Mac's and Mac would take his daughter's.

Well-respected or not, Owen's little girl was going to have to pay—for the loss of revenue to MCV and its employees, and for her father's stupidity.

Two

Olivia closed her eyes and inhaled. "I'm such a genius...."

"How long are you going to make us wait, Liv?" Tess asked, her stomach rumbling loudly. "I skipped breakfast."

Seated at the table, Mary Kelley stared at the tall redhead's trim belly, her brows drawn together. "Sounds like a train's derailing in there. Very ladylike."

Tess gave Mary a teasing glare. "Give me a break, I'm starving." She pointed to the massive yellow diamond engagement ring on her pretty blond partner's finger. "Not all of us have beautiful men bringing us poached eggs and bacon in the morning."

Smiling, Mary touched her growing belly, her blue

eyes soft and happy. "Ethan's very concerned about feeding his child. If I don't have something to eat every few hours he freaks."

Tess snorted. "That's just a little too sweet for me."

Mary laughed. "Oh, c'mon. You'll change your mind about that someday. Guaranteed."

"Doubtful. I'm too much of a loner—and I like it."

"Well, then we have to get you to go out and social-ize more." Mary's eyes lit up. "Maybe you'll meet someone at Ethan's and my holiday engagement party at the end of the month. He has some cute friends."

"No thanks."

"You might meet up with the right guy."

Tess shook her head and laughed. "I don't believe in the right guy, Mare. Now, a truckful of not-so-right guys—that's something I believe in."

Mary poured herself another glass of milk. "You're not old enough to be so cynical. How many men have you dated at twenty-five?"

"Enough to know better," Tess said seriously, then turned to Olivia. "You and I are lucky to have escaped the noose for so long, right, Liv?"

"Oh, so lucky," Olivia drawled as she cut squares of brownie. Olivia tried to ignore the wave of envy that moved over her heart as she recalled the tenderness in Ethan Curtis's eyes that morning when he gave Mary a goodbye kiss at the reception desk before leaving for his office. He had looked so in love, so happy, so over-the-moon excited about their baby.

Olivia didn't begrudge her friend the beautiful man

and solid relationship, but she did wonder if it was possible for someone like her to have half of that kind of happiness. In her heart of hearts, she wanted a man—someone to cook for and love and make babies with, but odds of that kind of life coming her way weren't great. Even though she had grown up in years, she was still very much stuck to the past. In many ways, she was still that depressed sixteen-year-old who had just lost her mother to cancer, couldn't get her father to notice her and had escaped from her pain in the most foolish ways possible—parties and boys and sex.

The shame of what she'd done and how many boys she'd allowed herself to be used by hadn't diminished in the ten years since, but in that time she had grown extraordinarily tough. She had also become cautious and resolutely celibate. Today, her reputation was lily-white—she was a hard-nosed businesswoman who kept the secrets of her past to herself.

"All right," Olivia said brightly, setting two extra large squares of chocolate brownie before Tess and Mary. "These will keep your mouths occupied."

"I believe she just told us to shut up," Tess said with a grin.

Mary picked up her brownie and sighed. "But it was in the very nicest way possible."

"True," Tess said, her pale gray eyes raking the gooey chocolate square. "And for another one of these I will not only give up on the guy and marriage talk, but if asked, I will gladly roll over and pant."

"Before you do," said a husky male voice behind them, "just be aware that you have an audience."

Mary and Tess whirled around in their chairs, and Olivia glanced up. Filling up the doorway with a cynical, though highly amused, expression was a man with eyes the color of espresso. He was tall and broad and was dressed impeccably in a gray pinstripe suit and black wool coat. Olivia found herself clenching her fists as she felt an irresistible urge to flip up the collar of his coat and use it to pull herself against him. The feeling was so out of character that it frightened the hell out of her and made her stomach churn with nervous energy. In the past seven years, since her self-imposed exile from sex, her body had rarely betrayed her. Sure, there had been a few late nights with a good romance novel in her bed, but other than that, nada.

As she looked at this man, every inch of her screamed *Caution!*

"Mac Valentine?" she said, relieved that her voice sounded steady and cool.

He nodded. "I think I'm early."

"Only by a few minutes," she assured him. "Please come in."

As he walked toward them, his stride runway-model confident, both Mary and Tess stood and offered him their hands. "It's nice to meet you, Mr. Valentine," Mary said evenly. "We were just enjoying a midmorning pick-me-up."

"I understand."

"Chocolate is life's blood around here," Mary continued warmly.

"I wondered what that amazing scent was the minute I got off the elevator."

Tess patted Olivia on the back. "Well, that's our resident chef's doing. Olivia makes magic and we all get to enjoy it."

His gaze rested on Olivia. "Is that so?"

Olivia shrugged good-naturedly. "I've never been good at false modesty, so I'll just say, yes, I'm a damn fine cook."

Amusement glittered in Mac Valentine's dark eyes, and Olivia felt a shiver travel up her spine.

"And on that note," said Mary, packing up the rest of her brownie and half-full glass of milk, "Tess and I will leave you in Olivia's capable hands. Welcome to No Ring Required, Mr. Valentine."

"Thank you."

Tess shook his hand again, then when his back was turned grabbed another brownie, before following Mary out of the room.

Trying not to laugh, Olivia watched Mac take off his coat and lay it over an empty chair, then she gestured to the table. "Please, have a seat." She snatched the orange platter of brownies off the counter and held it out in his direction. "Would you like one?"

He glanced up at her. "Do I have to roll over and pant?"

"Only if you want seconds."

Mac Valentine's eyes flashed with surprise at her quick comeback. "I'll let you know." Then he took a brownie from the plate.

She sat beside him and folded her hands primly. She

didn't know exactly why this man was here, but she had a feeling he brought trouble with him—several varieties of trouble. "Now, your assistant didn't reveal much about why you're here today when she made the appointment. Perhaps you could."

"Of course." He sat back in his chair. "I need you to turn my home into something far more 'homey' than what it is."

"And what is it?"

"A lot of unused space."

"Okay."

"I have clients coming in from out of town, and I want them to feel as though they've visited a family man, instead of a…" He paused.

She lifted her brows. "Yes?"

His lips twitched. "Someone who has no idea what those two words really mean."

"I see." And she did. It wasn't the first time she'd worked with a clueless millionaire playboy.

"I think it would be best if you saw my house for yourself."

She nodded, her gaze darting to the untouched brownie before him. "All right. But you understand my main area of expertise is in the kitchen."

"I was led to believe you were a multitasker."

Why wasn't he eating her brownie? "I am, but if it's true homemaking you're looking for then Tess might be a better—"

"No," he said, cutting her off.

She paused and gave him an expectant look.

"I want you," he finished, his face hard.

"Yes, I can see that," she said cautiously. "There's just one problem."

"And what would that be?"

"Your relationship with my father."

His brows lifted, just slightly. "I have no relationship with your father."

"He called me this morning and said you might be stopping by."

"Did he?"

"Yep."

Mac studied her for a moment. "You have the reputation of being a soft-spoken sweetheart, did you know that?"

"Are you trying to tell me that I'm not living up to my reputation?"

That query produced a wry smile from him. "I think I'm going to have a bite of this brownie now."

It's about damn time, she thought as she watched him slip the thick dark cake between his teeth. He had large, strong-looking hands and thick wrists, and she felt a humming in her belly as she wondered what he did with his hands that garnered him such a roguish reputation.

Her father had left her with a big warning about Mac Valentine. But instead of being worried she felt as curious as a one-year-old with an uncovered wall outlet in her sights.

"Good?" she asked, pointing to the half-eaten brownie on the plate.

"Very good."

"I'm glad," she said evenly. "Now, Mr. Valentine, why don't you tell me why you're really here?"

Three

If there was one thing Mac Valentine could spot a mile away, it was a worthy adversary. She may have been only a few inches over five feet with eyes as large and as soft as a baby deer, but Olivia Winston's cleverness and sharp tongue clearly declared her as a force to be reckoned with.

He hadn't seen that coming.

But then again, there was nothing he loved better than a challenge.

He watched those brown fawn's eyes narrow, and knew she would wait all day for the answer to her question.

"Due to circumstances beyond my control," he began, "my financial firm has lost its top three clients. I expect this to change over the course of the next few months when they realize that no one else in this town can make them the kind of money that I can, and did. But in the meantime, I need some help from you in landing a few heavy hitters."

Olivia's gaze flickered to the tabletop. "Do you need my help rebuilding your business or your reputation?"

"I see your father has done more than warn you about me." She didn't confirm or deny this, so he continued, "My business is not in any danger, but yes, my reputation has come into question and I cannot—and will not—allow that to continue."

"I see." Her smile turned edgy. "So, you want these potential clients to stay at your house instead of a hotel?"

"They're the type who appreciate home and family and soft edges—" he waved his hand "—all of that."

"But you don't."

"No."

She stood and took the plate that was in front of him, the plate with half a remaining brownie on it. "I have a question for you," she said, walking to the sink and depositing the dish there. She was small, but all curves, and when she walked it was seduction with every step. She turned to face him, leaned back against the countertop and crossed her arms over her full chest. Mac felt his gut tighten at the picture-perfect sight of her. "You believe that my dad caused your clients to leave your firm, right?" she said, arching her brow.

"Actually it was the lies your father spread that caused my clients to leave," he corrected.

"If you think that, then why would you want to work with his daughter? Unless…"

"Unless what?"

She walked to him and stopped just shy of his chair. If he reached out, grabbed her around her tiny, perfect waist and pulled her onto his lap, what would she do?

Whoever said payback was a bitch hadn't seen this woman.

"Unless you want to use me to get back at him," she said in a voice so casual she might have been reading a grocery list.

He matched her tone. "Is that what he told you?"

"Yes, but he didn't really have to."

"And how exactly would I use you?"

She shook her head. "Not quite sure." When she sat this time it was across from him.

"But your father has some ideas?"

"He's worried about your…" She smiled, thin as a blade. "Obvious charms—I mean, you're a great-looking guy. But I assured him he didn't have anything to worry about."

Well, this was a first. "Really?"

She nodded, said matter-of-factly, "I let him know that I would never be interested."

Mac felt his brow lift.

She laughed. "I don't mean to insult you, but the truth is, I would never go for a guy like you."

"Why do you think I'm insulted?"

The question caught her off guard and she stumbled with her words. "I, well—"

"And what kind of guy do you think I am?"

She lifted her chin. "One who assumes he can have anything he wants and any woman he wants."

Mac was not a man of assumptions, he was a man of words and deeds, and this woman was starting to piss him off. "I go after what I want, Miss Winston, but the people and things that come to me come at their own free will, I can assure you."

"You're just that irresistible."

He sat back in his chair. "Do all clients of No Ring Required go through an interrogation process or is it just me?"

"You're not a client yet, Mister—"

"Ah, Olivia." Tess stuck her head in the office, a confused expression on her face. "Can I see you for a moment?"

"Sure." Olivia turned to Mac. "I'll be right back, Mr. Valentine."

He saw, with vicious pleasure, that she was caught off guard and he couldn't help but grin as he said, "I wish I could say I was looking forward to it."

"If you can't wait…" she began.

"Oh, I can wait." He reached for his coat, and snagged his BlackBerry from the pocket. "I'll make a few calls."

Olivia felt like taking the man's phone and crushing it under her heel, but she smiled and nodded. Once out in the hall, the door tightly closed behind her, she faced her anxious-looking partners.

"What are you doing in there?" Tess said in a harsh whisper.

"Talking to a potential client."

"Insulting a potential client, is more like it," said Tess dryly, her arms crossed over her chest.

"Tess, you don't know the situation—"

Ever the mediator, Mary took over, her tone calm and parental. "Whatever the situation is, Liv, we could hear you all the way from our offices, and it sounded like an attack. Can you tell us what's going on?"

Olivia blew out a breath. "He's not a normal client. Hell, I don't even know if he's going to be a client at all."

"Not after what I just heard," Tess grumbled.

"At ease, Tess." Knowing her partners deserved an explanation, Olivia offered them the simplest one. "He and my father are in the same business, and a few of Mac Valentine's clients have decided to leave him and hire my dad instead. Mac thinks my father went the un-ethical route and told the financial community that he was doling out preferential treatment and tips to his better-looking clients."

"Wow," Tess began. "And did your father do that?"

"I can't imagine. My father's always been at the top of his profession. But the point is, Mac Valentine believes it. He thinks my father is responsible for the loss of three of his best clients, and now he's hiring me to get even."

Tess frowned. "What?"

"How?" Mary said, perplexed.

"I don't know yet, but I intend to find out."

"I don't like the sound of this," Tess said, shooting Mary a warning glance.

"Does he have a legitimate request for us?" Mary asked.

"He's out to bag a few new clients to replace the ones he's lost, and he wants me to make his house homey and inviting on several levels to impress them."

Mary put a hand on Olivia's shoulder. "If you don't feel you can handle him, Liv, Tess or I will—"

"No. First of all, he only wants me, and secondly, I'm not about to run from this man. I'm a professional, and I'll get the job done without getting involved."

Mary put a hand to her belly. "Sounds familiar."

"If I don't take the job, I'm willing to bet this guy would find a way of letting it be known around town that one of NRR's partners isn't a true professional. We don't need that."

Both Mary and Tess begrudgingly agreed.

"Just be careful, okay?" said Mary, squeezing Olivia's arm.

"Always." She gave them a bright smile and a wave and returned to the kitchen.

Mac was just finishing a call when Olivia eased back into her seat at the table, an NRR contract for him to sign in her hand. She took a deep breath. "Sorry about that."

"For leaving the room or for the insults?"

"Look, I'm going to take this 'job' because I am a professional and have partners who are counting on me. I'm also more than a little curious as to what you're going to try and pull. But know this, Mr. Valentine, lay one hand on me and we're done, understand?"

Mac looked amused. "For someone who believes herself so unaffected by a guy like me, you're acting worried."

"Boundaries and rules—good things to have."

After a beat, Mac agreed. "I understand. Now, can we get down to business?"

Olivia slid the one-page contract and a pen across the table. "When would you like me to start?"

"I'm having the DeBolds to my home this weekend."

"The diamond family?" She was surprised. The DeBolds would be a huge score and, according to her father, incredibly hard to land as clients. Mac Valentine had guts and drive, she'd give him that.

"They don't have children yet, but they are very into family, and the lifestyle that accompanies it. I need to make them feel at home with me."

She nodded. "I understand."

"I want home-cooked meals, family activities," he continued. "I want them to see me as secure, a man who understands their needs and desires for the future."

"Okay."

"And I'd like you to stay at the house with us."

She paused and stared at him, hoping her gaze was a cold as her tone. "No."

"In a room upstairs, down the hall from the DeBolds."

"And where will you be?"

"I sleep on the first floor."

Out of patience, she stood from the table and shot him a hot look. "It's not going to happen."

He ignored her as if she'd never said a word, "I want you to be there with us from breakfast to evening."

"Yes, I know. And I will."

In his ever-present calm way, he studied her. "All right, we'll discuss that particular detail at a later date. Now, on to something more important—this contract I'm about to sign, it guarantees confidentiality, is that right? You will not reveal anything about my business, and whom I do business with?"

"Of course." She had loyalties to her father, but her loyalties to the business and her partners came first. "Do you have menus in mind or would you like me to plan something?"

"I'd like you to plan everything."

After signing the contract and issuing a rather substantial check to NRR, Mac stood, towering over her like a statue. The soft scent of fading aftershave drifted into her nostrils and it annoyed her that just a small detail like his scent made her feel off balance. She found herself staring at his lips as he said, "I would like you to come by my house tomorrow, see what you have to work with and what you feel needs to be changed."

She stepped away from him, trying to regain her cool composure. "How's 10:00 a.m.?"

"You have my address?"

"Yes." She looked up at him and grinned slightly. "And your number, as well."

"Clever." He held out his hand, and for just a moment Olivia felt this odd sensation to turn and run from him.

But she knew how ridiculous and childish that thought was, and she confidently placed her hand in his.

There were no sparks or fireworks that erupted inside Olivia at that first touch. Instead something far more worrisome happened; she had an overwhelming urge to cry, as though she'd been on an island alone for ten years and had woken up to see a boat a few miles off shore—a boat she knew in her gut she wasn't going to be able to flag down.

She broke the connection first.

"Until tomorrow then," he said evenly.

She watched him walk out of the kitchen and down the hall, the edges of his wool coat snapping with each stride. Yes, it had been a long time since she'd met a man who affected both her mind and her body, and it was pretty damn unlucky that he happened to be an enemy of her father's.

Thankfully, she had become quite good at denying herself.

Four

Mac had hoped Olivia Winston would be moderately attractive. After all, it would make his goal a little easier and more pleasant to achieve if the woman he was going to seduce was decent-looking. Unfortunately this woman was miles past decent—circling somewhere around blistering hot. She was also intelligent and passionate and pushed sugar. And if he had any hope of seeing his plan through to the end, whenever he looked at her he was going to have to force himself to remember the he and her father were at war. And that her unhappiness and disappointment and permanent scarlet letter would be his justice.

He slowed his car to a comfortable seventy miles per hour as he exited the freeway. But seeing her as an enemy to be taken down wouldn't be easy. Damn, the way she'd looked at him with those fiery coffee-colored doe eyes, as though she couldn't decide if she was intrigued by him or wanted to follow her father's advice and toss him right out on his ass. Mac turned onto Third Street, Minneapolis's restaurant row. Eyeing the line of cars in front of Martini Two Olives, he backed into an open parking space with one effortless movement. Light snowflakes touched down on his windshield as he spotted a tall, cool blonde through the window of the packed restaurant.

She smiled warmly at him as he walked through the doorway. Mac gave her a kiss on the cheek, and above the din of celebratory restaurant patrons, he said, "Hello, Avery."

"Well, Mac Valentine, it's been way too long," she practically purred.

They took a table at the bar and ordered drinks. When a scotch neat was set before him, Mac asked, "How's Tim? You two still in love?"

Avery blushed and smiled simultaneously. "Blissfully. And planning on starting a family next year."

Mack leaned back in his chair and took a healthy swallow of scotch. "I'm a damn fine matchmaker. My best buddy and my firm's geeky ex-lawyer."

"Hey, watch it with the geek stuff. That was years ago. I'm a knockout now."

He grinned. "Yeah. You're all right."

She laughed. When her laughter eased, she grew

serious, her pale blue eyes heavy with sincerity. "You are a great friend, and you did a good thing. We owe you."

"Yeah, well, I never thought I'd have to collect on that debt, but times are a little…unsure."

"Tim mentioned something…"

"He always sucked at discretion."

"What do you need? Anything at all."

"Do you still represent the DeBolds?"

She nodded. "My favorite clients."

"I've heard they're shopping for a new financial firm, and I'd like to show them what I have to offer."

Her fingernails clicked on her glass. "They might've heard the rumors, Mac…. And you know how they are about family, or lack of. They don't want to deal with—"

"I know, I know. That's why I'm planning to be everything they're looking for and more."

She looked unconvinced. "Five-star restaurants and over-the-top gestures won't impress them. If you really want them to take the firm seriously, you'd need to do something—"

He put a hand up to stop her. "Let me tell you what I have in mind, then you can decide to set it up or not."

"All right," she said and lifted the glass of red wine to her lips.

Given the kind of man he was, Olivia had expected Mac Valentine to live in a sleek, modern type of home made of glass or stainless steel or something impervious to warmth. So it came as somewhat of a shock to find that the address he'd given her belonged to a stately, though charming, mansion on historic Lake of the Isles Parkway.

After parking in the snow-dusted driveway, Olivia darted up the stone steps and rang the bell, noting with a smile the lovely way winter's ravaged vines and ivy grew up one side of the house in a charming zigzag pattern. The wintry November breeze off the lake shocked her with a sudden gust, and she was thankful when the door opened. A tall, thin man in his late sixties ushered Olivia inside. He explained that he was the handyman, then told her Mac would be down in a minute. Then the man disappeared down a long hallway.

Olivia stood in the spacious entryway of Mac's home, staring at a beautiful, rustic banister and staircase, and wondering why it felt only slightly warmer inside the house than out.

"Good morning."

Coming down the stairs like Rhett Butler in reverse was Mac Valentine. He was dressed simply in jeans and a white shirt, the sleeves rolled up to reveal strong forearms. Awareness stirred in her belly. She liked forearms, liked the way the cords of muscle bunched when a man gripped something, or someone.

"Find the place all right?" he asked when he reached her.

"Perfectly," she said, noticing that not only did he look good, but he smelled good, too. As if he'd showered in a snowy, pine forest or something. Realizing her thoughts had taken an idiotic turn, she flipped on her professional switch and said, "Shall we get started?"

His eyes lit with amusement, but he nodded. "Come with me."

As Olivia followed him through the house, she noticed that each room she passed was more warm and inviting than the next, with wood paneling, hewn beams and rustic paint colors on the walls. But there was a glaring problem that Mac didn't mention as they walked—every room, from bathroom to living room to the fabulous gourmet kitchen, was bare as bones. There were no furnishings, no artwork, no tchotchkes—no nothing. It was the oddest thing she'd ever seen. It was as though he'd just moved in.

"I'm sensing a theme here," Olivia said with a laugh as they stopped in the kitchen. "You, Mr. Valentine, are a minimalist of the first order."

"Not totally." He gestured to a massive stainless steel contraption on the counter. "I have an espresso machine."

Two perfect cups of steaming cappuccino sat on the counter beside it. Olivia took one and handed the other to him. "And that's a good thing, but it barely strikes the surface of a family home." Her hands curled around the hot cup, feeling warm for the first time since she left the car. "I have my work cut out for me. What's up with all this?"

He shrugged. "I never got around to buying furniture."

It was more than that, she thought, studying him. It had to be. He hadn't put his stamp on anything. Maybe he hated permanence or didn't trust it. Whatever it was, it would be her first order of business. "How long has it sat empty like this?"

"I bought the place three years ago."

She nearly choked on her cappuccino. "That's just wrong. Where do you sleep? Or more importantly what do you sleep on?"

"I have a bed," he said, leaning against the counter-top. "Would you like to see it?"

"Absolutely. It's my job to make sure it has that stamp of family charm on it."

"What do you think is stamped on it now?"

"Debauchery?" she said quickly.

He grinned. "There's one more room down here, and in this one, I did put down a few roots. Two, to be exact."

Curious, Olivia followed him down a short hallway and through a heavy wood door. She stopped when she saw it and just stared. The room was, in a word, fantastic. Olivia walked in and stood in the middle, thinking she could hear music playing. One wall was made entirely of glass and she felt instantly at one with the white wonderland outside. Snow fell in big globs off the many tree branches and landed in pretty little tufts below. Birds hopped in the snow, making three-pronged tracks, and squirrels passed nuts back and forth. Inside, to her right were a pair of comfortable-looking navy-blue leather arm chairs that sat before a massive stone fireplace. Mac sat in one of the chairs and motioned for her to do the same.

"So once in a while you force yourself to relax?" she asked, as the heat from the blazing fire seeped into her bones and called upon her to relax.

"A man needs a refuge."

"Well, this is great."

He glanced over at her. "Do you think you can do something with this house?"

"I believe so."

"Good." He dug into the pocket of his jeans, pulled out a card and handed it to her. "Get everything. From sheets to picture frames. I don't care what you spend just make it warm and family friendly."

She stared at the platinum card. "You want me to furnish the whole house?"

He nodded.

"Every square inch?"

"Yes."

"Don't you want your stamp on it at all? Choices in artwork? Television?"

"No."

"I don't understand. Don't you want to feel comfortable here?"

"I don't like feeling comfortable—too much can happen to a person when they get comfortable."

"I'll try and remember that," she muttered.

His voice grew tight and cold. "All I want is the DeBolds, signed and happy."

Olivia was tempted to ask him just where he'd gotten such a desperate need to win, but it wasn't her place to care. He looked so serious, so raw, so sexy as he stared into the fire. Just his presence made the muscles in her belly knot with tension, and she knew that no matter what she told her father, after today, the truth was she was attracted to Mac Valentine. Not that she was going to do anything about it, or allow him to use her in any way, but the attraction was undeniably there.

"I'll do my best to set the stage, sir," she said with just a hint of humor.

He looked over at her then, his eyes nearly black in their intensity. "I hope so."

Her gaze dropped to his mouth. It was a lush, cynical mouth and for a moment she wondered what it would feel like against hers. She turned away. "You need to understand something," she said as much to herself as to him.

"What's that?"

"I know you didn't hire me because I'm a dynamite cook."

He snorted. "That's a little self-deprecating."

"No, it's the truth."

He didn't reply.

"You're looking for revenge. I'm not entirely sure how you're going to go about making me pay for something you believe my father did, but be forewarned…"

"Okay."

She forced herself to look at him. "I'm not going to fall under your spell."

"No?"

She shook her head. "Instead, I'm going to watch you."

"Watching me…I like that."

"And if you get out of line, I'm going to shove you right back in."

"Olivia?" He raised an eyebrow.

"What?"

"What if *you* get out of line?"

The question stopped her…from thinking and from a quick reaction. Mac saw her hesitate, too, and his dark eyes burned with pleasure.

"I think social hour has come to an end," she said tightly, standing. "I have a lot to accomplish in a short amount of time, so let's get to work. Show me the bedrooms."

"All of the bedrooms?" he said with a devious smile.

"Yes."

He stood, shot her a wicked grin and said, "Follow me."

Five

"So?"

"How was your meeting with Valentine?"

Olivia hadn't been back in the office more than five minutes and Tess and Mary were already standing in the doorway to the kitchen, their eyes wide with curiosity.

"Fine," Olivia said from atop a stepladder. She was searching through an upper cabinet, going through brands of cookware. She wanted to buy just the right one for Mac's kitchen. "I'm checking out a few things, then I'll be gone for the rest of the day."

They walked over and stood beside the counter. Tess asked, "What are you up to?"

"I have to furnish his house. The place is practically empty."

"The whole house?" Mary said, fingering the stainless fry pan that Olivia had set on the counter.

"Why do you sound so surprised? We've done similar jobs before."

"True."

Olivia could practically hear Mary's brain working. She glanced down. "What?"

"Are you furnishing his bedroom, too?"

"Oh, for goodness' sake. You have too many hormones running around in there."

Laughing, Tess grabbed a mug from the dish drainer and poured herself a cup of coffee. "We're just worried about you, that's all. If everything you said about this guy is true, he's up to more than just having you refurnish his house to bag a big client."

"Of course he is. I told you both that."

Mary put the pan down, grabbed Tess's cup and took a sip of her coffee. "What if he's having you design the bedroom he's going to try and seduce you in?"

"What? You're both acting nuts. He may be trying to use me, but he's incredibly clever and creative and interesting in his thinking. Whatever he's planning has got to be far more elaborate than—" She stopped at the worried looks on her partners' faces. "What?"

"You like him," said Mary.

"Oh, come on."

Tess nodded slowly. "You think he's 'clever' and 'creative,' and you probably think he's hot, too."

Olivia laughed and stepped down from the ladder. "Of course he's hot. Anyone with eyes could see the guy is hot."

"Oh, dear," Mary began, one hand to her belly as if she were protecting the baby from hearing anything too scandalous.

"Not good," Tess agreed. "I think I should take over the job."

"Will you two chill out?" Olivia grabbed a pen from her drawer and began writing down the names of several pieces of cookware. "Mac Valentine may be great-looking and charming and all the other things I said, but I'm not an idiot. He is also an arrogant womanizer with no furniture and no moral compass."

Tess nodded. "Yeah, that's pretty much what that article I read last week said. But somehow they made it sound like it was a good thing."

"What? What article?"

"Tess, go get it," Mary commanded, then turned back to Olivia.

"Oh, you read it, too," Olivia said.

Mary shrugged. "I was going through all the old magazines for recycle and you know how once I see something I can't stop reading, blah, blah, blah…" Tess returned and handed the copy of *Minneapolis Magazine* to Olivia. Mary said, "It's from a few years ago. Page thirty-four."

Letting out an impatient breath, Olivia grabbed the magazine and quickly flipped through the pages until she found the right one. And she knew it was the right one—not by the page number on the bottom right-hand corner, but by the enormous photograph of Mac and another man sitting on a stainless steel desk, a killer view of downtown Minneapolis displayed out the windows behind them. The spread was called "Workaholic, yet Woman Friendly," and featured both men holding BlackBerries in one hand and gold bars in the other. The sight of Mac, looking both handsome and arrogant as hell, didn't bother Olivia at all. It was the picture of the other man who sat beside him that had her stomach turning over.

Tim Keavy.

Her heart pounded furiously against her chest and she broke out in a sweat. The one guy from high school who knew what she truly was, knew her most shameful secret. God, did this mean that Mac knew, too? Was he going to use it against her? Against her father?

Olivia brushed a hand over her face. So much for her calm professionalism around Mac Valentine. Damn him. She hadn't expected him to go this route. She'd expected a full-out seduction—not using her past against her.

She stared at Mac's dark, dangerous face. Was it possible that he didn't know, that this was just an odd coincidence? A nervous shiver went through her entire body. She was going to have to be extra vigilant now. Watch every move he made and be prepared for it.

For a moment she thought about quitting the job, but she didn't run away from difficult situations anymore. She was no coward. She rolled up the magazine, then grabbed her notes. "I've got to go."

"Just watch yourself, okay," said Mary.

"I will." And on her way out the door she tossed the magazine in the trash.

* * *

November snow in Minnesota was said to be only the warm-up act for what was coming in January, but as Mac pulled into his driveway, his tires spinning and begging for chains as thick flakes of snow pelted his windshield, he wondered if Christmas had already come and gone without his knowing.

He pulled into the dry haven of his garage and shut off the engine. For a moment, he just sat there. He'd left the homes of many women before, but never had he come home to one. Yes, Olivia was an employee so it should have made the situation feel less domestic, but it didn't. He found her too pretty, too passionate, too smart to be just an employee.

When he entered the house a few minutes later, he heard the clanging sound of pots and pans being put away, and walked the short distance to the kitchen. His body instantly betrayed him as he spotted Olivia bending down, stacking pan lids on a shelf inside the island. Her dark hair was pulled back in a girlish ponytail and her pale skin looked flushed from all the activity. She wore a red sweater that hugged her breasts and waist, and jeans that pulled deliciously against her firm, round bottom. Devilish thoughts went through his head…like how good it would feel to be there when she stood up, to wrap his arms around her waist, to feel her backside press against him, to slip his hands under that soft wool sweater and feel her skin, her bones and her nipples as they hardened.

She turned then, caught him staring at her and gave

him an expectant look. There was nothing new in it, she sported this look quite often, but today there was something more in her eyes, as though she seemed to be silently accusing him.

He dropped his briefcase and keys and walked into the room. She'd done wonders. The space was perfect, homey, yet surprisingly modern with its green, gray and stainless steel accents. She had actually created a family kitchen for him, based on his tastes. She was damn good at what she did, and he couldn't wait to experience the aspect of the job were she had the most skill: the cooking.

"Well, Ms. Winston," he said, trying to lighten the mood. "You're going to make some man a great wife."

But the joke was lost on her. Her brows drew together in an affronted frown. "That was an incredibly sexist remark."

"Was it?"

"Yes."

"Why? I was giving you a compliment. The room looks amazing."

"So, only a husband can appreciate it?" she said, holding an incredibly large frying pan in one hand. "This is my job because I love it, not because I chose something stereotypically female. Okay?"

"Sure." He eased the fry pan out of her hand and put it on the counter. "This is not a weapon."

She stood a foot away, looking altogether too attractive, even in her ire. "I don't need stainless steel to do harm, Valentine."

He nodded. "I believe you." He reached up and brushed a stray hair off of her cheek. Her skin was so soft it made him ache to keep touching her. "Tell you what, when I go out back later and chop firewood you can say that I'd make a fine husband."

Not even a hint of a smile. He had no idea what he might have done to make her so mad at him, but he knew he was in trouble.

"I doubt very much that you chop wood," she said, picking up a pot from the sink. "But even if you did it would take a lot more than watching you to make me think that you'd be a good husband."

"Why are you so angry with me?" he said finally. "I could sense it the moment I walked in. You look damn pretty, but clearly pissed off."

"I'm not angry!" she shouted, snatching a dishtowel off the counter.

"What is it? Have a conversation with your father today?"

"Listen, buddy," she said sourly. "I don't need to talk to my father to get fired up about you."

"Fired up?" he repeated, amused.

"That's right." She put the pot on the stove top. "I am fully capable of forming my own opinions about you."

He stepped forward, making her step back, her hips pressing against the granite island. "And what have you come up with?"

"That you're a man who likes women—"

He chuckled. "Damn right."

"You didn't let me finish." Her voice was low, as intense

as her gaze. "So much so that you can barely remember their names five minutes out of the relationship."

"I don't have relationships, Olivia." He wondered if kissing her right now was a bad idea or a brilliant one. But she never gave him the chance.

"Are you proud of the way you're seen by other people?" she said. "Someone who jumps out of one bed only to charm his way into another?"

"That's the question of a woman who is in desperate need of a man in her bed."

She stared at him, her cheeks red and her dark eyes filled with irritation, then she dropped her dishtowel and walked out of the kitchen. "It's getting late."

"I'll walk you out," he said, following her to the front door.

"Don't bother." She grabbed her coat and hat and gloves and purse and opened the door. "I'll be back first thing in the morning."

Then Mac saw the snow and remembered his drive home. "Wait. It's really coming down out there."

"Good night, Mr. Valentine."

"The roads are pretty bad."

She stepped out the door and went down the path, calling back, "I'm a Minnesota native, Mr. Valentine. I've driven in worse than this."

"Damn it to hell!"

Olivia glanced over her shoulder and winced when she saw that she'd backed over Mac's mailbox. There it was, stretched out in the snow, a sad, black pole with a missing head. What a fool she was thinking that just because she had four-wheel drive and an SUV she could avoid the realities of Mother Nature. She'd just wanted to get away from that man, out of his house and the questions about how others saw him, how he had jumped from one bed to the next and all of that crap that she'd tossed at him—questions she was really asking herself.

She put her car in gear and stepped on the gas. A sad whirring sound was followed by rotating tires.

"Damn snow."

She slammed the car back into Park. This job had gone from a leap of curiosity to just plain complicated. Never had she acted so unprofessionally, and even though Mac's motives for hiring her were questionable at best, her job was to execute without getting personal, without allowing her fears to drive her actions. Well, from this point on she was going to make sure that happened.

She cranked up the heat, then reached for her cell phone and dialed information. But before the automated operator picked up, there was a knock on her window. Startled, she turned to see Mac, in just his jeans and shirt, and she pressed the button for the window.

"What are you doing?" he asked.

"I've killed your mailbox, I'm stuck in the snow and now I'm calling a cab."

He cursed, the word coming out in a puff of breath. "You'd do better to call a tow truck. No cab's coming out in this. I could brave it and try to get you home, but I don't think that'd be very smart."

"No, it wouldn't," she agreed. "You should go back

inside." She rolled up the window, then reached for her cell phone and dialed the operator once more.

Mac knocked on the glass, hard this time. Again, she rolled down her window. "What?"

"You're going to freeze."

"Only if you keep making me roll down the window. Now, go in. You're the one who's going to freeze in that getup, and I refuse to be responsible for your getting pneumonia or hypothermia or something."

"You're acting like a child. Come inside."

"I'm not acting any way. I'm being sensible. It's not a good idea for me to go back in there tonight. Things got too heated earlier."

"True, but I think we could use a little more heat in that house."

"It's too cold for jokes." She sighed. She just wanted to get home, into the tub and have a hot soak, maybe watch a few reruns of *Sex and the City*.

But that wasn't going to happen.

"It's your choice," he said, his teeth chattering now. "Nice warm fire or freeze in the car."

She heaved a sigh. "Fine. I'll come inside…but I'm going to call for a tow truck."

He helped her out of the car, and she followed him through the drifts of snow to the walkway, then up to the front door.

"If the tow truck can't get to you tonight," Mac said as he opened the door, "you are welcome to stay in my room."

She stopped inside the entryway. She wanted to scowl at him, but instead she laughed. "Are you insane?"

"Actually I thought I was being pretty gentlemanly." He turned back and grinned. "And that's a rare thing for me."

"Can I use your phone? My cell doesn't work very well in here."

"Sure." He took her coat and hung it up, then covered her hands with his and slipped off her gloves. A shot of awareness moved through Olivia, from the hair on her scalp to the backs of her knees, and she looked up to find him watching her, his dark eyes intense. He took off her gloves so slowly it made her belly knot with tension, and when her fingers were finally released from the warm leather, he took her hands and squeezed them into his cold palms.

"You're freezing," she said.

"And you're warm." His fingers laced with hers, and her muscles tensed. "I don't think I'm going to let go."

Sadly, she didn't want him to, but she wasn't about to give in to herself or to him. He was using her, and she'd allowed herself to be used too often in the past.

Olivia pulled her hands away. "I'm going to make that call now."

"You're not getting your car out tonight, Liv," Mac said evenly. "Now I'm going to be bunking in one of the leather chairs by the fire since all the rest of the bedrooms haven't been furnished yet, so if you do stay, take my bed—or don't take it. Either way, I won't bother you."

She didn't know if she believed him, but what could she do? She needed the shelter for tonight. "Thank you."

He nodded. "Good night." Then he walked in the direction of the den.

Six

The guy at the first tow truck company hung up on her, the guy at the second tow truck company actually laughed when she'd asked if he could come out and excavate her car, and her third call had gone straight to a machine.

Olivia had known it would be somewhat of a long shot to get home tonight, but after the way her body had reacted to Mac's touch earlier—a very simple, not that overtly sexual a touch—she was really hoping.

She sat on the edge of Mac's king-sized bed, her shoulders drooping forward. She was tired and cold, and disappointed in herself for caving in and taking his room. A better woman might have stuck to her guns about not bunking in Mac's sparse, octagon-shaped room, maybe grabbing a few extralong towels from his bathroom and cuddling up on the carpeted floor of one of the empty guest rooms. But she was a wimp that way. She liked her creature comforts. She'd always wondered about people who liked camping. Strange noises and bugs for bunkmates…what was the attraction? Anyway, she was sleeping in Mac's bed tonight. She just hoped he'd keep his word and wouldn't venture out of the den to find her.

She pulled the comforter off the bed and wrapped it around herself. Then again, why would he leave such a lovely, warm spot by the fire? Olivia blew out a puff of air to see if she could see her breath. It was cold as hell in Mac's house, a ridiculous kind of cold that sank deep into your bones and could only be relieved by a hot bath. She didn't know what that handyman did around here, but first thing tomorrow, she was calling in a professional heating technician. Forget all the warm, family friendly furnishings. If the house felt like an igloo, the DeBolds were going to head straight for the nearest five-star hotel.

Olivia thought about lying down and trying to sleep, but when nature called, she threw off the comforter and dashed into the master bathroom. And there she saw it—surrounded by beautiful pale brown tumbled stone was a massive box of glass with a rain showerhead above and four body sprayers along one wall. Oh, she wanted to cry it looked so inviting.

Did she dare? Maybe just a quick one? Just to get warm.

Feeling a sudden burst of happiness at the thought, she flipped on the water and turned the temperature knob to the equivalent of "hotter-than-hell." After closing the door to keep all the beautiful heat contained, she got undressed. She was just about to step inside the shower when she heard a knock on the bedroom door.

Her heart dropped into her stomach. No, no, no. Not now. Why was he here? Did he have radar or a sixth sense that told him when there was a naked woman in his room or something?

She snatched a huge white bath sheet and wrapped herself in it, then she opened the door and walked out into the frigid air.

He was knocking again. "Olivia?"

She opened the door just wide enough to accommodate her head, but hid the rest of her from his view. "Yes?"

"So you took the room?"

"Yes. I took the room. Can we not make a big deal out of it?"

"Of course." He grinned. "Are you okay?"

"Fine. Just tired." *And cold.* "What's up?"

He didn't look convinced. In fact, he was trying to assess the situation as he spoke. "I put a frozen pizza in the oven if you're interested."

She shook her head. "Thanks, but I'm not very hungry. Just tired. Very, very tired."

"All right. Good night, then." Olivia thought that he was about to leave, that she was about to finally get warm, but then he paused and cocked his head to one side. "What's that?"

"What's what?" she asked innocently, as if she didn't know.

"Is that water running?"

"No."

His mouth twitched. "Are you taking a shower?"

"Not at this precise moment," she said with irritation, which caused him to grin, full-on and slightly roguishly.

"Taking advantage of my steam shower, are you?"

She rolled her eyes. "Oh, for God's sake."

"Hey, I don't blame you, the thing is awesome."

"Well, good…then I'm going to go—"

"Have all the towels you need?" he asked.

"Yes."

She looked expectantly at him. Time to leave, Mr. Valentine. What more was there to say? After all, he'd humiliated and humbled her, what could be left? But he didn't leave, he just stood there looking sexy in his black sweater and pants.

Olivia let out a frustrated breath. "I'm freezing, okay? I need a way to warm up."

His grin widened, his gaze dropped. "No, too easy."

"Good night, Mac," she said through gritted teeth. "Enjoy your pizza."

He chuckled and pushed away from the door frame. "All right. Enjoy your shower. But," he said as he turned to walk away, "if you find that you can't sleep or you get hungry, you know where to find me."

"That, I can promise you," she called after him, "will never happen."

Mac put another log on the fire, then rescued his bottle of beer from the rutted mantel before dropping back into his chair. The book he was reading was pretty dull, but he was halfway through it and he wasn't a quitter. Just as he was about to find out why early man and an anthropoid ape had almost the same number of cranial bones and teeth, he heard footsteps behind him.

"You suck, Valentine."

Mac chuckled and turned around. "Now why would you say something like—" The words died on his lips as he caught sight of her, practically glowing in the firelight. From the moment he'd seen Olivia Winston, serving up brownies and attitude in her office kitchen, he'd found her incredibly attractive. Tonight, however, she was breath-stealing.

Her white blouse was untucked and rumpled, and resembled a man's shirt with the cuffs falling loose about her hands. Her long, black pants seemed a little too big without the heels and belt, but it was her face and hair that had his pulse running a race at the base of his throat. With no makeup, she looked fresh, delectably soft, her flawless skin glowing a pale peachy color. Her long, damp, dark hair swung sexy and loose, and reminded him of a mermaid. It took every ounce of control he had not to take her in his arms and kiss her until she realized just how perfectly their bodies would fit together.

She walked over and dropped into the chair beside him. "My hot shower wasn't so hot."

"No?"

She tossed him a look of mock reproof. "And it's all your fault."

"I did inadvertently ask if you wanted me to join you," he reminded her, taking a swallow of his beer.

"That's not what I mean."

"No?"

"You made me stand at the door talking to you so long the hot water was almost gone by the time I got in there."

"I'm sorry," he said sincerely. "Let me make it up to you with a never-ending fire and a cold slice of pepperoni."

She looked unconvinced at first, then she shrugged. "Okay." She took a piece of pizza from him and practically attacked it. "Oh, the fire feels so good. Your room is freezing, Valentine. This house is freezing."

"It can get a little cold, I guess."

"You sound like you don't mind turning into an ice cube every time the sun goes down."

"I hardly notice. I'm really only here to sleep."

"Well, first thing tomorrow I'm calling a heating technician. The DeBolds may sell ice, but they don't want to sleep in it."

He grinned at her. "That was funny, Liv…clever."

She shrugged. "I have my moments," she said, reaching for a second slice of pizza.

Mac grabbed another bottle of beer from beside his chair, opened it and tipped it her way. "Something to drink?"

"Sure, why not?" She took the cold bottle from him. "Thanks."

"You bet."

"Sitting in a freezing house in front of a fire eating

cold pizza and even colder beer—this night couldn't get any stranger, could it?"

He sipped his beer, then said, "How about if I tell you that when I was around nine or ten I thought—well, I'd hoped—I'd grow up to be a comedian."

She turned to stare at him. "That would be stranger."

"Hard to believe, I know. I'd put on one of my foster father's suits and tell incredibly awful jokes to these three crazy dogs they had. I was really into toilet humor at nine."

"You grew up in a foster home?" Her tone had changed from cute sarcasm to barely disguised pity in a matter of seconds.

He hated that, and rarely told anyone about his less-than-ideal beginnings to avoid hearing just such a reaction. He didn't know why he'd just blurted it out to her. Inadvertently, yes, but still… Maybe he needed to ease up on the beer. "I lived in a few foster homes. No big deal."

"What happened to your parents?"

"My mother died when I was two, and my father was never really in the picture."

She bit her lip. "That's tough."

He shrugged. "It wasn't that bad."

"Was the foster father you borrowed the suit from a good guy at least?"

"He wasn't awful. Although he did come home early one night to see me knocking around in that suit and he was pretty pissed off."

"What did he do?"

"Went for the belt."

Olivia's mouth dropped open. "What a bastard. What a cowardly piece of trash. If I had been there I would've kicked his—"

Mac's dark laughter cut her off. "It was no big deal. It happened." Even though he said the words with cool casualness, he appreciated her passion and protective nature. "You know, twenty-five years ago, there wasn't this push for fathers to be loving and gentle. 'Hands-on' had a different meaning." He took a healthy swallow of beer. "Every kid got boxed by their dad, foster or not, once or twice while they were growing up."

She sat forward in her seat, and looked at him with a strange mixture of sadness and care in her eyes. "No, they didn't."

Sure, he'd had a few beers, but he understood exactly what she was saying, and who she was saying it about. His jaw twitched. Owen Winston may have disciplined with words, but he was certainly no saint. "Well, I learned my lesson," he said tightly. "I never touched his suits again."

They were both quiet for a while after that, both drinking their beer and staring into the fire. Mac's ire subsided, and he was close to sleep when he heard her say his name.

He turned his head. "Yeah?"

"What happened to the career in comedy?"

He chuckled. "Ended shortly thereafter."

She smiled. "Bummer." Her cheeks were flushed from the heat of the fire and she looked really beautiful.

"Or a blessing—depending on how you look at it."

Yawning, Olivia curled deeper into the chair. "Well, feel free to try out any new material you've got on me."

His body stirred with her words, but he said nothing. He wasn't going to push things. Whether she wanted to admit it to herself or not, she was growing interested in him, attracted to him, and someday soon he would have her in his bed. It wouldn't make nearly the impact if he took what she wasn't ready to give. Owen Winston needed to know that his sweet, innocent little girl had come to Mac all on her own.

Mac heard her breathing grow slow and even, and after a few minutes, he closed his eyes and allowed himself to sleep, too.

Olivia woke up in a daze. In front of her the dying fire crackled softly. For a moment, she thought it was morning, but with a quick glance to the windows to her left she saw that the inky blackness of night had yet to turn to the steely gray of dawn.

"Hey."

She looked over at Mac, who was sitting forward in his chair, his dark eyes seductive and hungry under heavy lids. "What time is it?"

"Around three."

She blinked a few times, feeling foggy. "I should go back to bed."

"But it's cold in there."

"Yeah." But she didn't move. She just stared at him.

Mac got out of the chair and went to her, sat on his

heels in front of her. The hot flicker in his gaze made every bit of Olivia's tired limbs feel on edge and alive.

He reached up to touch her face. She grabbed his wrist, that hard, thick, oh-so-masculine wrist, and he stopped and stared at her. Her heart thudded in her chest as he leaned in, his gaze hungry, his mouth so close. Looking back on that night, Olivia had wanted to blame the foggy tiredness in her brain or the cold and snow for what she did next. But she knew exactly why she went temporarily nuts. All the frustration she felt at her attraction to Mac, and all the years of pushing aside her feelings of need and desire, just seemed to explode in her face at that moment.

Her hand snaked around his neck and she pulled him down for a kiss. And not a peck kiss, either, but a full-blown, lip-nuzzling, teeth-raking, breath-stealing kiss.

Seven

"Holy—" Mac didn't finish the end of the curse as he took her in his arms and dropped back onto the rug, taking her with him.

Poised above him, Olivia welcomed the crush of Mac's mouth and the heat of his body against hers. It had been so long, almost ten years since she'd been touched like this, felt a man's lips on her, his warm breath mingling with hers. The delicious hard angles and clean scent of his skin thrilled her, and she pushed away any thoughts of how wrong the situation might be.

She threaded her fingers in his hair and gripped his scalp as he changed the angle of his kiss. Soft, hot, drugging kisses. All she wanted was to get closer to him, feel a new kind of heat, forget who she was for a few minutes, forget what he was after.

In one easy movement, he flipped her onto her back. The warmth of the fire made her sweetly dizzy and she arched against him. Sensing her need, Mac explored further. His hand moved down, under her shirt, and she felt his palm on her belly. Little zaps of fear warred with the almost desperate urge she had to feel his fingers brush over the skin of her breasts, hear his breathing change when he cupped them and felt the weight of them, feel the lower half of him grow thick and hard as his thumb flicked back and forth over her nipple.

Mac dragged his hand up, over her ribs and along the side of her rib cage. She arched and tilted her body toward his hand, silently begging him to go there, put her out of her misery or show her exactly what misery felt like again as he gave in to her fantasy.

He was no fool, he knew what she was asking for and he delivered with the utmost care. As he applied teasing kisses to her lower lip, his hand drifted from her ribs to her breast, and slowly—so slowly—he began to roll the hard peak between his thumb and forefinger. Olivia shuddered, and released an anguished sigh. Oh, such sweet torture. She felt as though she had just been plunged into a deliciously hot bath, and God help her, she never wanted to step out of it.

But somewhere, deep in the back of her mind, she knew if she didn't, she was going to drown.

He left her mouth and dipped his face into her neck, kissing and suckling her rapid pulse as the speed of his fingers on her nipple quickened. Back and forth, faster and faster.

Her legs were shaking now, almost uncontrollably, and she knew if he didn't stop touching her, she was going to climax. Right then and there without him even going near the hot, wet place between her thighs. And she couldn't do that—not now, not for him.

She pushed at his chest and sat up, her breathing as labored as if she'd just outrun a hungry animal.

"Why are you stopping?" His voice was ragged.

"You know why," she uttered softly.

He raked a hand through his hair. "Damn it, Liv, there's nothing wrong with being together like this, taking what you need when you need it."

She looked down at him, her body warring with her mind. "From you, there is." He looked so sexy lying there in the light of the fire with his hair tousled and a light shadow of beard around his full mouth. "From a guy who's just using me—"

"You're using me, too," he uttered darkly. "Don't pretend you're not. I could feel every moment you've denied yourself in your touch, in your kiss, the way your hips pushed against mine. You're starving, Olivia, and you want to feed so badly you're still shaking with it."

"I'm cold."

"Bull. It's hot as hell in here right now."

His words startled her. She did want him, but she wasn't altogether sure why. Was it to use him? Was it to make up for lost time and to finally feel a release in her body and a release of the past? Or was it because she was actually starting to like him?

Her body still hummed from his touch, but she ignored it and said softly, "I'm going to go back to your room now. Alone."

"Is that really what you want?"

Of course it wasn't, but she needed to step back and gain some perspective here. "Yes."

"All right. But if you get cold—"

She stopped him right there and stood. "A little cold might be a good thing right now." And without another glance in his direction, she left the room.

Mac woke up to the sounds of a snowplow and his doorbell chiming. Looked as though the streets were clear and his furniture delivery had arrived. He pushed himself out of his chair and stretched, the kinks in his back protesting. As he walked to the front door he wondered if Olivia was still asleep in his bed or if she'd slipped out at dawn.

He raked a hand through his hair. What kind of trouble would he be in if, after he let the furniture guys in, he went to wake her up, started at her ankles and worked his way up? He grinned, the lower half of him tightening at the thought. She might kick him out of bed—but maybe not.

Mac was still very deeply ensconced in that fantasy when he opened the front door. But when he saw who was on the other side, all softness and desire vanished, and his fangs came out. "Hell, no. It's way too early for this."

Owen Winston looked ready to murder him. "Where's my daughter?"

"You have a helluva lot of nerve coming here."

"Where is my daughter?"

Mac leaned against the doorjamb and raised one eyebrow. "In my bed."

The older man's eyes bulged out like a tree frog's and he lunged at Mac.

Eight

Olivia walked down the hall, an aching stiffness in her bones that came from sleeping in a chair for most of the night. If she'd had the day to herself, she might grab a massage and a whirlpool bath at the local spa, but she had a full plate today and a good soak in her bathtub when she got home tonight was about the best she could hope for.

When she got to the stairs, she heard voices below in the hall. "Oh, that's my cab," she called to Mac. "The tow truck company said they should be pulling out my car later this afternoon, so you don't have to—" She stopped talking. The voices she heard were angry and threatening, and she recognized them at once. One belonged to Mac, and the other, she was pretty sure, belonged to her father.

She raced down the hallway, but when she got to the entryway, all she could do was stare. There was her father, his back against the wall, looking like he wanted to kill Mac with his bare hands. And Mac, who was standing in front of him, only inches away, looked just as menacing.

"What the hell are you two doing?" she demanded. When neither of them answered, she walked over and stood in front of them, her hands on her hips. "Mac," she said evenly, trying to bring some sense of calm to the situation, and to the two fire-breathing men before her. "Take a breath and back up."

His jaw flickered with tension, but he didn't look at her when he muttered hotly, "Yeah. Sure. As long as your father here doesn't jump on me again."

"What?" Olivia turned to her father. "Jump on you?" When Owen didn't look at her, she put a hand on his shoulder and said in a voice laced with warning, "Dad, what are you doing here?"

Owen's lips tightened as he turned to look at her. "We need to talk."

"You could've called me."

"I tried to call you, but you weren't at home."

"Let's go outside." Embarrassed at her father's behavior, and the overly parental way he was treating her at that moment, Olivia tried to smooth things over with Mac. She felt really awkward looking at him, especially after their encounter last night, but she forced herself to. "I'm sorry about this—"

Mac put a hand up. "Don't worry about it, just get him out—"

"Don't apologize to him, Olivia," Owen said with a sneer. "He's a monster, a conniving—"

Before Owen could hurtle any more insults Mac's way, Olivia took his hand and pulled him out the door, calling over her shoulder, "I'll be back at ten for the delivery. If you'll just put a key under the mat…"

Not expecting a response, Olivia led Owen down the walkway toward her waiting cab. She was furious, and could barely contain her anger. She understood her father's need to protect her, but this was way over the top.

As soon as she believed herself to be out of earshot, she faced him, her tone grave. "Dad, seriously, what are you doing? Coming here and attacking a man in his own home?"

"He's no man, he's a—"

"He could have called the police. Hell, he still could…and I have to say I wouldn't blame him. What were you thinking?"

Owen suddenly looked very weary as he reached out to touch her hair. "I was trying to protect you, honey, stop you from making a huge mistake." His eyes clouded with sadness. "But it looks like I'm too late for that."

"Too late for what? What mistake…?" Then she understood why her father had come. She heaved a sigh. It was the same old thing—her father's desperation, and constant fear that she was going to turn out like his older sister Grace. Her poor aunt Grace, who had been way too wild, made way too many mistakes and had been totally incapable of picking a decent guy. Poor Aunt Grace who, after staying out until dawn partying with some jerk from the local college, had been killed in a car accident on her way home. She'd just turned eighteen the week before, and Olivia's father had never gotten over losing her.

Olivia understood her father's fears and his need to protect her, but she wasn't sixteen anymore. This over-protectiveness needed to stop.

Standing beside the open door of the cab, Owen was shaking his head. "That monster stood there in his doorway and smiled when I asked him where you were."

Oh, great. "What did he tell you?" As if she needed to ask.

"That you were in his bed." Her father said the words as though he had acid on his tongue.

So Mac had baited her father. What a shocker. God, they were both acting like such juvenile idiots….

"Is it true then?" her father asked, his brown eyes incredibly sad.

"Dad, I'm not going to answer that."

The cab driver opened his window. "You going to be much longer, lady?"

Olivia shrugged. "I don't know—maybe."

The man rolled his eyes and closed his window.

"Olivia, please," her father continued. "You're such a good girl. Don't act irrationally—and with a man who only wants to use you to get back at me."

"I'm not acting irrationally, Dad. And I'm not a girl anymore."

"I know…."

"No, I don't think you do." She bit her lip and contemplated broaching the subject about his fears and what the hell had happened so long ago. But his eyes still spit fire and he looked way too closed. "Listen," she said gently, "you knew I was taking this job, and that it would mean working closely with Mac Valentine."

"Helping my enemy."

"I have a company to run, too."

Owen seemed to consider this, then he said in a slightly calculating tone, "Okay, so you're helping him do what exactly? Go after new clients?"

Olivia shook her head. "That's confidential."

Owen looked livid. "The man is a conniving bastard who wants to hurt you, and you're worried about…"

She put a hand on his shoulder. "How long have I been living on my own, supporting myself?"

"Since you were eighteen." He pointed at her. "But that was not my choice."

"Exactly. I'm a grown woman who makes her own choices, and as I've told you before—respectfully—I don't have to answer to you or to anyone."

Owen wilted slightly, but it wasn't the first time he'd heard her speak this way. After her mother had died, and after Owen had emotionally checked out, Olivia had made decisions for herself. Some of them had been downright stupid, even reckless, but the majority, she'd been proud of—like her business.

Her father's gaze grew soft as he looked at her. "What happened to my little girl?"

"I left her back in high school." Olivia leaned in and kissed him on the cheek. "I have a busy day, as I'm sure you do, too." She got into the backseat of the cab and gave him a little wave before her driver backed out and pulled away.

Mac stood in the living room, watching Olivia's cab take off down the street. The glass on every window in the house was pretty thin, and he'd heard their entire conversation. Looked like he had gotten it wrong; Olivia may not be that sweet, naive girl he assumed her to be. But where her father didn't want to deal with it, Mac burned to know every detail of the past she seemed to be hiding—especially after last night.

Grinning, he left the living room and went into his study. Embers burned in the fireplace, and as he sat in one of the leather armchairs, his body twitched with the memory of Olivia in his arms, on top of him, underneath him. The way she'd responded to his touch, the silent, hungry demands. She'd felt pleasure before, but she'd been denied it for way too long. There was no need to push her, he realized. The demands of her body had started to take over her good sense and Mac was going to be there, totally available when it happened again.

After all, her father thought him to be a womanizing bastard, and Mac was ready to prove him right.

All in all a very successful day, Olivia mused, walking from one beautifully furnished room to the next. She'd quite outdone herself, and in record time, too. Each room complemented the next in leather and iron, glass and walnut.

She stopped in the living room and marveled at the classic, comfortable feel of the space. Not to mention the warm air puffing from the vents in the baseboards. She'd finally found a guy to come out in the snow and turn on the heat. A vast improvement in and of itself.

Though she'd purchased all the linens for the upstairs, the bedroom furniture wouldn't be arriving until early tomorrow morning. But they were close—well on their way to creating a very modern, very homey, very Mac-like environment.

"Ms. Winston?"

Olivia returned to the living room where Dennis Thompson, a local art gallery owner who looked rather like a short version of Ichabod Crane, was hanging several paintings she'd purchased for Mac's house.

"What do you think?" he asked, holding up two Josef Albers pieces, both in several shades of yellow. "On top of one another?"

She sat on the new distressed, brown leather couch to get a better view. "Hmm…I don't know. How about—"

"Side by side?" came Mac's voice behind her.

Dennis Thompson looked behind Olivia and beamed at Mac. "Perfect. I'll just go get my tools from the car."

Olivia turned, surprised. "You're home early, Mr. Valentine. Are you here to supervise?"

He was dressed in a tailored black suit and crisp white shirt, his tie loosened from his neck. "I came home for a late lunch or an early dinner."

"Oh, really?" she said with a grin. "I haven't stocked

the fridge yet and you ate the only frozen pizza, so what were you planning on having? The cocktail onions or that last, lonely bottle of Corona?"

He walked around the couch and sat beside her. "You're a pretty good chef, aren't you?"

"I like to think so." He smelled so good. She tried not to breathe through her nose.

"Well, then, can't you make something amazing out of onions and beer?"

"No," said Olivia succinctly, lifting an eyebrow. "Can I ask you something?"

"Shoot."

"When do you normally leave the office to come home?"

His lips twitched. "Oh, I don't know…"

"Approximately."

"Seven, eight…nine, ten."

She looked at her watch. "It's four-thirty—why are you here?" Her heart began to pound in her chest as she wondered for a moment if he was there to see her. After what happened that morning with her father, she wouldn't blame him. She just hoped he wouldn't spread the story around town. "Are you going to fire me?"

"No." He laughed. "That's over and done with." His voice turned serious. "As long as it doesn't happen again. I can't have your father showing up when the DeBolds arrive."

"It will not happen again," she assured him. "You have my word."

Satisfied with that answer, Mac leaned back and

crossed his arms over his chest. "I'm not exactly sure why I'm here. But I think the reason might be embarrassing."

"For you or me?"

"Me. Definitely me."

"Oh, well, then share, please."

He glanced around the room. "It's really warm in here."

"I know. I had the tech come this morning and it took him hours just to—"

"No, I mean what you've created here from the furniture to the artwork to all those little things on the tables and in the bathroom and on the mantels. It's all warm. I never thought I'd be comfortable with warm.…" He looked at her, surprise in his gaze. "As you start to make my house into a livable, family-friendly place I sort of want to be here to see it…and you."

Her muscles tensed at his words and she could almost feel the pressure of his lips on her mouth once again. Her reaction to him, her attraction to him, wasn't going away, she knew that. But she hoped that maybe the two of them could forget what happened last night and go on about their business.

When she found his gaze once again, Mac had that look in his eye, that roguish one that made her knees weak and her resolve disappear.

"Listen," she began, "about last night…"

"Yes?"

"I was half-asleep."

"Before or after you kissed me?" he asked huskily.

Right. Her brow creased with unease. "As clichéd as this is about to sound, it'll never happen again."

He grinned. "Are you sure?"

"Yes."

"We made sparks."

His words and the casual way he offered them made her laugh. "I won't argue with that. You're one helluva kisser, Valentine, but…" And on that note, she sobered. "You're also using me." She put a hand up as she saw him open his mouth to speak. "I know you think I'm using you, too, but I'm not. And last night, I didn't."

His grin evaporated. "Then why…"

She stared at him, wondered what he would say if she told him she was starting to like him—that even with the information she had about him and why he'd hired her to begin with, she believed he was good man. A damaged man—but, under that hard-ass exterior, a good one.

"Ms. Winston?"

Dennis Thompson had returned from his car and was standing in the doorway with his toolkit and another painting. "I'm sorry to interrupt, but before we can hang the rest of the pieces, we need you to tell us where you want them."

"I'll be right there," she told him before facing Mac again. "Now, we have guests arriving tomorrow afternoon, and I have to finish up here, then go home and plan a menu."

He nodded. "Have you decided to stay here?"

"Not yet."

"If you do, I won't bother you."

"I'm not worried about you starting anything." It was all she had to say. The flush on his neck and the stiffness in his jaw were obvious clues that he'd heard the slight emphasis on the word *you* and understood her meaning all too clearly.

She got up and was about to leave the room when Mac called her back. "Olivia?"

"Yes?"

"As far as the menu, I've invited another couple to join us tomorrow night, so there will be six instead of four."

"Okay. Anyone I know?"

He shook his head. "I don't think so. It's the DeBolds' attorney and her husband."

"Got it." She tossed him a casual, professional smile, then left the room.

Nine

If someone called Mac Valentine an arrogant jerk to his face, he usually agreed with them before kicking them out of his office. He was arrogant. But in his defense he believed he was the best at what he did and that unshakable confidence was the only way to stay at the top of his game. Today, at around three o'clock in the afternoon, he'd had that theory tested and proven correct by one of the clients who, just a few weeks ago, had been running scared after Owen Winston's foolish attempt to discredit him. After waiting for twenty minutes in the lobby, the client had sat before Mac and had practically begged him to take him back. Whether the man still believed that Mac had given preferential treatment and tips to his other clients or not, being at a competing firm had not proved lucrative and he wanted back in.

Mac pulled into his garage feeling on top of the world. When one client returned, he mused, the others would surely follow—they'd leave Owen Winston and other financial firms and come back to where they belonged.

He cut the engine and grabbed his briefcase and laptop. Today's success would by no means deter him from getting revenge on Winston. And in fact, he actually felt a stronger desire to follow through on his plans with Olivia. By the end of the weekend, he thought darkly as he stepped out of the car and headed into the house, he would have it all: Owen's little girl and a powerhouse of a new client to add to his roster.

The heavenly scent of meat and spices, onions and something sweet accosted his senses when he walked through the door. Home sweet home, he thought sarcastically, walking into the kitchen. But once there, he promptly forgot everything he'd just been thinking, plotting and reveling in. In fact, as he took in the sight before him, he realized he had little or no brain left. "You look…"

Olivia stood before the stove, stirring something with a wooden spoon. "Like a wife?"

He saw the lightness, the humor in her eyes, but couldn't find a laugh to save his soul. He cleared his throat, his gaze moving over her hungrily. "I was going to say, breath-stealing—but I suppose you could look wifely, as well."

She wore pink. He hated pink. He'd always hated

pink. It was for flowers or cotton candy. But Olivia Winston in pink was a whole different matter. The dress she wore was cut at the knee and cinched at the waist, and pushed her perfectly round breasts upward, just slightly—just enough so that she looked elegant, yet would also drive a man to drool. Her long dark hair was pulled up to the top of her head, causing her neck to look long and edible, and her dark eyes, still filled with humor, reminded him of warm clay beneath long, black lashes.

And she had wanted him to forget about the other night? Get serious. All Mac wanted was to pull her against him, ease the top of her dress down, fill his hands with her, play with one perfect pink nipple while he suckled the other. His groin tightened almost to the point of pain. He wondered, would she moan as he nuzzled her? Or would she cry out again, allow herself to climax this time?

"Well, thank you for the compliment," she said, gathering up several bottles of wine. "Would you mind setting those things down and giving me a hand?"

"Sure. What do you need?"

She nodded in the direction of the island. "Wineglasses. Can you grab them and follow me?"

He picked up the spotless glasses that were laid out on a towel on the island and followed her into the dining room.

"Well, what do you think?" she asked, setting the bottle down on an impressive black hutch.

This woman wasn't fooling around. She was damn good at what she did, and it showed in every detail.

She'd set the table with unusually modern-looking china, gleaming stemware and silver silk napkins. But the most impressive part was the centerpiece, which sat in the middle of a round walnut table. It looked as though she'd brought the outdoors inside with cut branches from his yard, white candles and small silver bells.

He set down the wineglasses and released a breath. "It's perfect."

"Good." She checked her watch. "Your guests will be here in thirty minutes. You'd better wash up and change your clothes."

"I have time."

She gave him an impatient look. "It would be rude, not to mention awkward, if you weren't here when the doorbell rings."

"Careful, or someone might think you're the woman of the house," Mac said with amusement, wondering how long it would take to kiss that pink gloss off her mouth.

Reaching for the dimmer switch on the wall, Olivia lowered the lights a touch. "For all intents and purposes this weekend, I am."

His gaze swept over her. "Did I tell you how much I like the color pink?"

"No, you didn't," she said primly, putting her arm through his and walking him toward the stairs. "But we really don't have time for that now. I have a dinner to get on the table, and I won't allow anything to burn."

He grinned. "Of course, can't have things getting too hot now, can we?"

She glared at him, raising one perfectly shaped eyebrow. "I think a shower would be good for you."

He nodded and said with sardonic amusement, "Yes, dear," then took the stairs two at a time. She was right. He needed a shower, a really cold shower. Hell, he thought, chuckling to himself, he might do better diving into one of those piles of snow burying his lawn.

Harold DeBold was one of those guys people just liked the minute they met him. Hovering somewhere around forty, he was very tall and thin, and had pale blond hair and wintery blue eyes. He reminded Olivia of a surfer, relaxed and free-spirited. His wife Louise, on the other hand, was dark-skinned, dark-eyed, completely city-sexy in her gorgeousness and totally high-strung. But she also seemed sincere, and when she was told that Olivia was going to be their chef for the weekend, instead of thinking it odd that the person Mac had hired to help him was not going to stay in the kitchen and/or serve, but was going to eat and socialize with them, she'd acted as though it were the most normal thing in the world—even adding that she was thrilled that Olivia was going to cook some down-home Minnesota fare for them.

"Honestly," the woman said to Olivia, curling her diamond-encrusted hand around her wineglass. "I feel like all I've eaten for days is foie gras, caviar and squid ink. I'm over it."

Chuckling, Harold told Mac, "We've been in New York for the past week."

They were waiting for the DeBolds' attorney and her husband to arrive as they sat in Mac's den, which had been completely transformed into a contemporary, masculine, but family-friendly retreat with his two existing leather chairs and several other pieces of dark blue chenille furniture curled around the fire. Cozy rugs dressed the hardwood floor, and lights had been installed outside to showcase the wintery-forest view from the floor-to-ceiling windows.

Mac reached over and topped off Louise's wine. "You two were in Manhattan for a week and you didn't get around to pasta?"

Louise snorted. "Unfortunately, no."

"Next time you go, let me know," Mac said seriously. "There's this tiny hole-in-the-wall in Little Italy that you've got to check out. The spiciest pasta puttanesca—not to mention the best-tasting parmesan cheese I've ever had."

"Cheese." Chuckling, Harold said with dramatic flair, "City folk think that all us backcountry Wisconsinites get to eat is cheese, so they refuse to take us anywhere that might serve it. Instead, they figure they've got to impress us with all those fancy, unpronounceable, unrecognizable *foods*." As he said the last word he mimed air quotes.

Olivia held out a tray of hors d'oeuvres. "Well, everything you're going to eat tonight is as easy to pronounce as it is to eat."

Louise sipped her wine and said, "Thank God."

Harold took one of Olivia's famous blue cheese

jalapeño poppers wrapped in bacon and practically sighed when he ate it. "Oh, my," he said to Olivia, his blue eyes so warm she couldn't help but wonder if he was flirting with her just a little bit. "If these are any indication of your culinary skill, then you might never get me to leave."

Louise agreed. "These tomato basil tarts are over the top."

Olivia smiled, pleased that her fun and flavorful finger food was such a hit. "Thank you."

"Are you self-taught, Olivia?" Louise asked.

"I actually went to culinary school, then I worked for several chefs in town before starting my business."

Harold's brows drew together. "And what kind of business is that exactly? Catering? Or are you a personal chef?"

Olivia looked over at Mac, who was sitting in a dark blue wing-back chair by the fire. He didn't appear concerned by the question, and even winked at her, so she was as honest as she needed to be. "Myself and two other women provide catering, decorating, party planning…those kinds of services to clients."

"And are your clients mostly clueless men or women?" Louise asked, her eyes dancing with humor until she realized she was including her host in that question. She offered him an apologetic smile. "Of course, I didn't mean you, Mac."

Mac laughed. "No apology necessary—I know where my skills lie and they're not in the kitchen."

"Mine, either, sadly," Louise said on a sigh.

"All it takes is a little practice," Olivia told Louise sympathetically.

Harold shook his head wistfully. "She has tried, Olivia."

"Hey, there." Louise gave him a playful swat on the arm.

The doorbell chimed over the laughter in the room, and Mac stood. "I'll get that. Must be Avery."

When Mac was gone, Harold turned to Olivia. "My lawyer and her husband are great people, and are usually very punctual."

Olivia smiled warmly. "We're in no rush tonight."

"I like that attitude," Louise said, snatching up another tomato tart. Male laughter erupted from the front hall, and Louise rolled her eyes. "Boys. We just found out that Mac went to college with Tim, fraternity buddies or something."

It was as if time slowed after Louise had said the name *Tim,* and Olivia couldn't seem to find her breath. Even the room spun slightly. "Tim?" she managed to say. "That's your attorney's husband?"

Louise may have answered her, but Olivia's ears were buzzing. It wasn't him. It couldn't be him.

"Sorry we're late," came a voice that Olivia recognized at once. She swallowed. What was in her throat? It felt like a rock. She wouldn't turn around—couldn't turn around. He was coming and she felt frozen to the couch.

"Avery couldn't decide on which shoes to wear," he said dryly.

"Don't you blame me, Tim Keavy, you know it was your fault." The woman sniffed and added, "The Vikings game was on."

"Typical." Mac chuckled. "Avery, Tim, I'd like to introduce our amazing chef for the evening."

No…. She didn't want to.

"Olivia?" Mac said.

She wasn't ready….

"Olivia?" Mac said louder, sounding puzzled now.

Her heart slamming against her ribs in a noxious rhythm of fear and dread, Olivia turned around to see the one person in the world who knew her secret—the boy who, nine years ago, had walked in on an affair between a teacher and a student. A boy who had made a young Olivia Winston feel like trash from that day forward.

Ten

For a moment, Mac wondered if Olivia was having an anxiety attack. Her face was as pale as the snow outside the window, and her eyes looked watery, as though she desperately wanted to cry, but wouldn't allow herself to go there in front of guests.

What the hell was wrong with her? Had the DeBolds said something to upset her while he was gone? The quick, almost fierce anger that rose up inside of him surprised him, as did the protective impulse jumping in his blood.

Protecting Owen Winston's daughter was hardly the plan.

His gaze shifted, and he saw Tim staring at Olivia, his lip drawn up in a sneer. It was a look Tim usually reserved for people who didn't perform to his standards, from office staff to the guy who continued to put whipped cream on his espresso at the local coffee shop. Mac didn't get it.

He watched Tim walk toward her and stick out his hand. "Wow," he said coolly. "Olivia Winston. Small world."

"Microscopic." Olivia rose stiffly and clasped his hand for about half a second. "Hello, Tim."

"How do you two know each other?" Mac asked, though the tone of his voice sounded slightly demanding.

"We went to the same high school," Tim stated flatly.

"How funny," Louise remarked with a dry laugh, clearly not seeing the discomfort between the two. "You knew Olivia in high school and Mac in college?"

"That's right," Tim said.

Mac watched as Olivia seemed to get herself under control. With a smile affixed to her face, she walked over to Tim's wife and held out her hand, "Hi, I'm Olivia. Welcome."

"Avery Keavy. It's so nice to meet you." Avery had the good sense to leave the high school talk alone, and instead gestured to the coffee table and assorted hors d'oeuvres. "These look amazing. I'm sorry we're late."

Olivia picked up a tray and offered a stuffed mushroom to Avery. "It's no problem. Dinner's almost ready. In fact, I'm going to check on it right now. If you'll all excuse me…" After she placed the tray on the buffet, she excused herself and headed for the door.

"Need any help?" Mac called after her.

She turned then and glared at him. "No. I've got everything under control, Mr. Valentine."

Mac had never seen anyone look at him with such full-on revulsion, and he had no idea why. And her palely masked anger didn't end there. It continued all through dinner. Not that the DeBolds or the Keavys really picked up on it, they were way too focused on the food—which was perfection. But Mac saw every little glare she tossed his way as he served himself another helping of her mouthwatering brisket and smashed red potatoes, and wondered why the hell she was so upset at him. It couldn't be just because he was responsible for inviting Tim to the house. What was the big deal, so he knew her in high school?

Maybe he'd have to go to Tim for the information if Olivia wasn't going to speak to him. He looked over at Tim. The guy was just going with the flow. He didn't even look at Olivia.

"Pecan pie is one of my favorite desserts," Harold was saying to Olivia, his plate nearly empty.

Olivia gave him a warm smile. "I'm so glad. Would you like a second piece? How about you, Louise?"

"Absolutely." Louise held out her plate. "And I'm not even going to ask you to force me in to it."

Avery dabbed her mouth with her napkin. "Will you force me then, Olivia?"

"Of course," Olivia said, keeping her gaze fixed on Tim's wife. "I demand that you hold out your plate, Avery."

Avery gave her a small salute. "Yes, ma'am."

Avery and Louise broke out into laughter as they

passed around the fresh whipped cream to top their pie. Mac, however, was too distracted to find humor in the situation. When he should've been selling himself to the DeBolds, talking about how he could change their financial future, he was staring at Olivia, wondering what was wrong with her and how he could fix it. It pissed him off. Why did he care if she was angry with him?

After the brown-sugar coffee and pecan pie had been completely devoured, Avery thanked both Olivia and Mac for their hospitality and she and a very unsocial Tim took off. The DeBolds, feeling a little jet-lagged and extremely full, requested an early night, as well, and retired to their room.

The night had been a successful one—on the business front at any rate. The DeBolds seemed content and happy with Mac and with his home, and wasn't that the first step to having them as clients? With the DeBolds in bed, Mac had to deal with Olivia, who had fled to the kitchen as soon as both couples had gone.

When Mac entered the room, Olivia was camped out over the sink, washing dishes at a frenetic pace, taking out her anger on a serving platter.

"Great dinner," he said, walking over to her, leaning against the counter next to the sink.

"Yes," she said stiffly. "I think you've impressed them."

"I hope so."

"Yep. One step closer to getting the big fish on the hook."

He didn't respond to her sarcasm. "Do you need any help?"

"No."

He exhaled heavily. "Are you going to tell me why you're so angry with me?"

She continued to scrub the life out of a white platter, and Mac wondered if talking right now was a stupid idea. Maybe she just needed to cool off with her soap and hot water. But then she dropped the platter in the sink and turned to face him, anger and disappointment in her dark eyes.

"I knew you were out to punish my father and use me in the process," she said. "But I had no idea how far you'd go."

"What are you talking about?"

"Are you kidding me?"

"No."

"Tim Keavy," she snapped.

"What about him?"

She shook her head. "Don't do that."

"Do what?"

"Don't act like you're clueless. It doesn't suit you. You're a shark, be proud of it."

"You're nuts, lady." He gritted his teeth and pushed away from the counter. "All I know is you two went to the same high school."

"Right." She glared at him, her nostrils flaring. "So how does this go? You think by outing my sordid past to my dad, he'll back down on whatever he has on you? Apologize?" She shook her head, then walked past him out of the room, saying, "It'll never happen. My father's even more stubborn than I am."

He followed her. "Where are you going?"

"To my room."

"You're not leaving?"

"I'm going to give this job everything I have, get you the clients you want, then get the hell out. You'll have no ammunition if you're looking to ruin my business reputation along with my personal one."

"You're talking crazy," he said, following her up the stairs and down the hall to the guest room. She had chosen the one on the opposite side of the house than the DeBolds, and Mac was thankful he didn't have to whisper.

When she got to the door, she said, "Good night, Mac," then went inside.

When she tried to close the door behind her, he wouldn't let her. He held the door wide. "Listen, you can't just throw all that garbage in my face, then walk away."

She released her grip on the door, put her hands up in the air. "What do you want to say, Valentine? That you didn't know your best friend from college knew me?"

"Damn right," Mac said hotly, walking into the room and closing the door behind him.

"I don't believe you."

"I don't care if you believe me or not, it's true."

Standing just inches from him, she held her chin high as she stared hard into his eyes. "It's going to take a lot more to humiliate me and screw with my father than tossing my past mistakes, my past humiliations, back in my face."

He grabbed her shoulders. "I'm not doing that."

"Bull."

"I don't give a damn about your past."

"I do!" she shouted, her voice cracking with emotion. She dropped her gaze, bit her lip and cursed. When she looked up at him again, she looked like a kid, so vulnerable it killed him. "I hate that part of my life."

Tears sprang to her eyes.

"Stop that." He gave her a gentle shake, for the first time feeling the guilt that came with his plan. "Stop it, Olivia."

This wasn't how it was supposed go. He was the one who was supposed to make her miserable, then send her back to her father in shame. He should be reveling in the fact that he had access to information about her past that would make her father suffer.

"Damn it." He hauled her against him and kissed her hard on the mouth. "I don't care what happened before, and neither should you." He nuzzled her lips, then nipped at them, suckled them, until she gave in, gave up and sagged against him.

"There's nothing wrong with this," he said as his hands found her lower back and raked upward. "Or this." He dipped his head and kissed her throat, suckling the skin that covered her rapid pulse, grinning as a hungry whimper escaped her throat. "Nothing to be ashamed of, Olivia."

"You don't understand," she uttered, letting her head fall back.

He held her close, his lips brushing her temple. "Help me to, then."

"I…can't. I made a promise to myself.…"

He rubbed his face against her hair. "When you were a kid?"

"Yes," she whispered.

"You're a woman now." He nuzzled her ear, nipped at the lobe. "Everything's different."

On those words, she froze. "That's the thing," she said, her voice hoarse. She drew back, her eyes filled with regret. "Nothing's different. Not at all. I refuse to make any more stupid mistakes with men who just want to…" She didn't finish, just shook her head.

"Olivia."

She disentangled herself from his grasp. "Two more days. That's it. That's all you're getting from me, so do your worst because after this weekend is up you're going to be done. Done with me and done with my father."

"We'll see about that," Mac said darkly before turning and leaving the room.

Eleven

And the winner of the worst night's sleep contest was…Olivia Winston.

Standing over the stove, she made sure her pan was hot, then carefully cracked an egg into the hole she'd made in the slice of crusty bread. Three cups of extra-strength coffee and all she wanted to do was go back to bed. But maybe that had nothing to do with being tired as much as it had to do with hiding. For someone who had gone into this job thinking it would be easy-peasy, she sure was going through a lot of difficult, trying moments. Not to mention, some sexually charged moments that she couldn't get out of her head. She'd really underestimated Mac and his desire to bury her father, and she'd overestimated herself, and her needs, in the process. She'd wanted to find out just how Mac was going to get back at her dad, and had basically given him the goods to make it happen.

She flipped the bread. To make matters worse, she wanted more—more of him, more of his touch, his kisses. She was weak and a total disappointment.

She felt him in the kitchen even before she saw him, and wanted to kick herself for the giddiness that erupted inside her at the thought of seeing him again.

"Good morning."

She spared him a quick smile. "Morning." He looked good, Saturday-morning sexy in expensive black sweats and dark tousled hair.

"Sleep well?" he asked, pouring himself a cup of coffee.

"No. You?"

He chuckled. "I slept okay."

"Yeah, guys can sleep through anything. Your brains turn off—so lucky."

"Maybe our brains turn off, but that's about it." Despite his hard, unyielding business-guy attitude, he had this obvious sensuality, this slow, tigerlike laziness that made him seem always ready for bed. "Honestly, the effects of what happened in your room last night are still with me this morning."

She ignored the pull in her belly. "Me, too—but maybe in a different way." She laid another slice of bread in the hot pan and cracked an egg. "Listen, Mac, I don't know if I believe what you said last night about Tim—if you set that up or not—but I can't worry about it anymore. I've spent too many years worrying about the past. Can we just let everything go and concentrate on what we're trying to accomplish with the DeBolds?"

"Let *everything* go?"

"Yes. Do you think you can do that?"

"Do you really think *you* can do that?" he countered, his eyes glittering with heat.

Before she could answer, Harold and Louise walked into the kitchen, all smiles and dressed like models from a Hanna Andersson catalog. "Morning," Harold said, taking a seat at the island.

"Morning," Mac said good-naturedly. "Sleep well?"

"Perfect," Harold said. "Something smells good, but that's not surprising."

Olivia glanced at Mac, who was watching her over his steaming cup of coffee, then she turned to her guests. "Eggs in a blanket, bacon and good, strong coffee."

"Are you trying to fatten us up?" Louise asked, sitting beside her husband.

"Of course," Olivia said on a chuckle, setting two cups of coffee before them. "But only so you have all the energy you need for what I have planned today."

"And what do you have planned?" Mac asked, seeming to suddenly realize he'd never discussed plans with her.

Olivia looked at them all brightly. "Ice skating."

Mac practically choked on his coffee. "Ice skating?"

Louise, on the other hand, looked as though she were about to explode with happiness. "Did you hear that, Harold?"

"I did. I did."

Clasping her hands together like a little girl, Louise cried, "I haven't been skating in ten years."

"Well, then maybe it's not such a good idea—" Mac began, but Louise cut him off.

"Not a good idea? No, no, no—it's perfect. Harold and I had our first date on a skating rink. Rounder's Pond—it was in back of my grandfather's property, a beautiful kidney bean shape and surrounded by trees. Do you remember that, honey?"

"Of course." Harold smiled at his wife, then looked over at Olivia. "You have made my wife very happy today. Thank you."

"My pleasure." Olivia beamed as she turned back to the stove. "Now, let's get you two fed."

Mac came to stand beside her.

She whispered over the DeBolds' loud chatter, "You look panicked."

"And you look happy about that," he muttered.

Laughing, she took two perfectly cooked eggs in blankets out of the pan and placed them gently on plates. She whispered, "Buck up, Valentine. Ice skating is perfect and fun, and I've planned a lovely picnic afterward with hot chocolate."

"I don't skate, Olivia."

"Well, you lucked out then." She handed him the two plates and smiled. "I'm a great teacher."

He'd been good at sports. Not the school kind. You had to spend more than a year living in one place to get on an organized team, but he'd killed at street basket-

Play the Lucky Hearts Game

and get...

2 FREE BOOKS and
2 FREE MYSTERY GIFTS...
YES! YOURS to KEEP!

Yes! I have scratched off the silver card. Please send me my *2 FREE BOOKS* and *2 FREE mystery GIFTS.* I understand that I am under no obligation to purchase any books as explained on the back of this card.

Scratch Here!
then look below to see what your cards get you...
2 Free Books & 2 Free Mystery Gifts!

► DETACH AND MAIL CARD TODAY! ►

326 SDL ENUW   225 SDL ENNM

FIRST NAME

LAST NAME

ADDRESS

APT.#

CITY

STATE/PROV.

ZIP/POSTAL CODE

(S-D-11/07)

Twenty-one gets you
2 FREE BOOKS and
2 FREE MYSTERY GIFTS!

Twenty gets you
2 FREE BOOKS!

Nineteen gets you
1 FREE BOOK!

TRY AGAIN!

Offer limited to one per household and not valid to current Silhouette Desire® subscribers. All orders subject to approval.
Your Privacy – Silhouette Books is committed to protecting your privacy. Our Privacy Policy is available online at www.eHarlequin.com or upon request from the Silhouette Reader Service. From time to time we make our lists of customers available to reputable firms who may have a product or service of interest to you. If you would prefer for us not to share your name and address, please check here. ☐

The Silhouette Reader Service™ — Here's how it works:

ball and alley soccer in every community he'd been sent to. He'd never tried hockey though, and before today had assumed that hockey, or anything involving skates, was a little like trying to understand German when all you spoke was Spanish. But he'd jumped into it with both blades. It took him about twenty minutes to really feel his balance, but after that, he was like a demon racing on the ice, even getting an impromptu hockey game going with Harold and some of the guys on the lake.

After an hour, he retired himself and joined Olivia on the bench. She was dressed all in white and looked very pretty. She'd spent much of her time with Louise in the center of the lake, teaching the woman how to execute perfect little turns and spins and other girlish things Mac didn't have a clue about—but he'd sure liked watching her in between plays.

"Well," she began, her cheeks pink from the cold and exercise, her eyes bright with humor. "You sure took to that like a baby to a bath."

"You think so?"

"You had the moves, Valentine. I was very impressed."

Instead of throwing away her compliment with a laugh, he felt an odd sensation in his gut as if he'd eaten something past its expiration date. And he knew exactly what that feeling was—he'd felt it once or twice in his life and it worried him. He liked this woman.

He blew out a breath, turned to watch Harold and Louise as they skated casually around the lake. He had to get rid of this feeling, stop himself right here, right now, before he did something stupid like abandon his plans to make her father pay. He had one more night—tonight—to get her in his bed, then they were done.

"And I'm impressed," he said in a voice he normally reserved for his employees, "with your skills off the ice."

"What do you mean?" she asked, looking confused.

"You did well." Mac gestured toward the DeBolds, who were laughing and holding hands as they weaved in and out of the other couples in the "slow lane." "They look happy."

"They do," she agreed.

"Funny that you picked the very thing they did on their first date."

"Not funny at all."

He stared.at her. "You knew?"

She smiled.

"How—"

"Romance breeds comfort, comfort breeds trust," she explained, taking out a thermos of hot chocolate and pouring them both a cup. "And that's what you're looking for, right? Trust in you and your skill?"

He shook his head. This woman was unbelievable. He'd had no idea how far she'd go to help him. Honestly, he hadn't expected much with her knowledge of what his true motivations were, but she'd really come through for him. Too bad he couldn't offer her a position in his company. He asked her, "How could you find out something like that? Even if you researched them, something so personal…"

She laughed as she handed him the steaming cup of

chocolate. "You really didn't know who you were hiring, did you? Silly man."

"Maybe not—but I see it now. I see you."

"Yeah? What do you see?" she asked, sipping her chocolate.

"You're a damn good wife."

"Thank you."

"And if I wasn't completely against legal unions, I might be compelled to make you marry me."

She laughed again, clearly thinking that every word he'd just uttered was a nonsensical joke. Mac wasn't so sure.

"That's very flattering, Mac, but you know I'd have to turn you down."

"Really?"

"Yep." She looked away, sipped her chocolate.

"You want me to ask why, don't you?"

"Nope."

"Fine," he grumbled. "Why?"

She turned back to face him, the humor in her gaze now gone. This time he saw the sad reality of a woman who knew and understood him—it wasn't pretty to look at.

"What?" he said. "Go ahead, say it."

"I don't think you'd make a very good husband."

Nothing shocking there. "Well, I don't know. Last night you thought—"

"That was passion, desire," she interrupted.

"You can't have passion and desire in a marriage?"

"Of course, but those kinds of needs are only *part* of

it." She nodded toward the middle of the lake. Louise was now teaching Harold how to do a spin. He looked like an idiot, Mac thought. An idiot in love.

"Look at them," Olivia said wistfully. "They're friends, true companions. They really like each other."

Mac pressed his lips together. Not that he wanted to admit it—and he wasn't about to, out loud at any rate—but he liked Olivia. He thought they made a pretty good team.

"They're coming back," Olivia said, pulling Mac from his thoughts. "And after a full morning of cold and exercise, I'm betting they're hungry."

"I know I am," Mac said softly, his gaze resting on Olivia.

She shook her head at him, but he saw that flash of hunger in her eyes—the same one she'd worn last night when he'd touched her, kissed her.

Screw friendship. Maybe what they had wasn't long-lasting, but it was real, and there was going to be a moment when she allowed herself to take it. And if he was on top of his game, that moment would come tonight.

At four o'clock in the afternoon on Saturday, Olivia was dealt some bad news. She was in the kitchen, pounding chicken breasts into thin paillards, when Mac walked in and announced, "Harold and Louise want to ask the Keavys to come over after dinner tonight for cocktails."

Olivia's heart dropped into her stomach with anvil-like heaviness. She continued to smash the chicken, but with slightly more vigor. "Okay."

"Avery's the DeBolds' attorney. It's good to have her here. I think it will get them talking and asking questions tonight, and I need that to happen. They're leaving in the morning, so—"

"You don't have to explain, Mac," she said tightly, not looking at him. "This is your home. You don't need my permission to invite someone here."

"I know that." He sighed, pushed a hand through his hair. "Damn it, I care about your feelings, okay? Too much, but there it is."

"You don't need to worry about me." She needed him to just stop talking about it, stop asking questions. But that wasn't Mac's way. "I'm a professional. I will not allow my feelings to distract from the goal of this evening."

"Screw that. What happened with Tim? Did he treat you badly? Not show up on a date? Was he…all over you on a date? What the hell happened between you two?"

"Nothing."

"I'm trying to be sensitive here, Olivia, because I can see that whatever happened in the past is upsetting to you—but it was high school. That's a long time ago."

Her head came up and she glared at him. "You've got to stop with the questions. This is none of your business, Mac."

"I know, but if it interferes—"

"It won't. I swear I'll be the perfect hostess tonight— I was just caught off guard before."

He looked as though he wanted to say more, ask more, demand more, but after a moment he turned and started to leave the room.

Thinking he was gone, Olivia faced her meal-in-progress once again, feeling tired. All she wanted to do was throw her ingredients into the garbage and go home, forget about Tim, forget about Mac. She put down her mallet, took off her plastic gloves and put her head in her hands.

"Olivia."

Her heart sank. Damn him, why hadn't he left the room like he was supposed to? He'd seen her break down, lose it a little, and that wasn't good. She felt him beside her.

"I'm just a little tired, that's all," she said.

"Come on. It won't go further than this room, if that's what you're worried about. I swear I won't use anything you tell me. Talk to me."

She looked up and melted at the concerned look on his face…she could almost believe it was genuine.

He reached for her, wrapped his arms around her. "Give me something, Olivia."

Maybe it would be easier if he knew, she thought. Then it would all be out in the open—he wouldn't have to dig for information. But…there was a part of her that didn't want him to know, didn't want him to see her as Tim had seen her, and maybe still did—as trash, as a little tramp who had been so starved for love she'd slept with her teacher.

"He knows something about me," she began, letting her head drop onto Mac's shoulder. "A mistake I made. And he didn't like me for it, simple as that." She couldn't go further than that, she just couldn't….

"Simple as that, huh?"

"Yes."

"I don't believe you."

She stepped back, lifted her head and gave him a bold smile. "I have chicken to prepare."

"Olivia…"

"Everything will be fine tonight, Valentine."

He reached out and brushed his thumb across her cheek. "You're sure?"

His touch was like the best kind of comfort food and she wanted to wrap her arms around him again and beg him to take away her anger over a past she couldn't find a way to change. But that job belonged to her alone. If she ever wanted to feel comfortable about men and sex and love again, she had to deal with her past herself. "Now, I want you to get out of my kitchen and go be with your guests. It's your last night to impress the DeBolds, and I'm going to make sure you do."

Mac regarded her without smiling. "It's their last night, and it's your last night."

She nodded, then faced the counter again and got back to work. She wasn't sure when he left exactly, but when she turned around to get the arugula from the fridge, he was gone.

Twelve

The amazing thing about Olivia Winston was that once she made up her mind not to care about something or someone, it came rather easily. When Tim and Avery joined them after dinner for drinks and a few games of Pictionary, Olivia put her nerves aside and became the professional she knew herself to be. She was in her element: a small, elegant, relaxed, family friendly get-together with great desserts and just enough spirits to make everyone smile. She and Tim had managed to successfully ignore each other and the DeBolds were happy and acting exceptionally warm and familiar with Mac.

An all-around success.

"We've had such a good time," Louise said, sipping

a second cup of Olivia's delicious hot-buttered rum as they relaxed beside the fireplace in the den.

Harold nodded in Mac's direction. "You're a class act, Valentine."

"Thank you, Harold." Mac tipped his glass in the couples' direction. "It's been a pleasure having both of you here. Maybe we can do it again over the summer."

Harold grinned warmly. "Maybe. Maybe."

Avery had excused herself to go to the ladies' room, and perhaps Tim had felt uncomfortable without her, but he, too, excused himself to have a cigar on the porch.

While they were gone, Olivia asked Louise about her New York trip and if they'd seen any Broadway shows, and as she listened to the woman's hilarious accounts of a show they saw about underpants, she saw Mac get up and follow Tim out of the room.

Her stomach rolled over, but she forced her attention back on Louise.

He was a guy. A hardheaded guy who went after what he wanted regardless of the consequences. And right now what he wanted were answers.

He knew where his friend had gone—the balcony off the kitchen—and headed straight there.

Out in the inky darkness, a light snow was falling and the air felt still and frigid. Tim was simultaneously puffing on his cigar and shaking from the cold.

Mac stepped out onto the balcony, barely feeling the below-zero temperatures. "I couldn't stand those things when we were in college and I can't stand them now."

Laughing, Tim said curtly, "Then why are you out here?"

"I need to talk to you."

"About what?"

"About her. What did you do to her?"

His nose was red at the tip, his ears, too. "What? Who?"

"Olivia," Mac said impatiently. "In high school. What happened between you two?"

"Oh, man…" Tim shook his head.

"Come on."

"I don't want to go into this," Tim said, tossing his cigar over the balcony and into the snow.

"You will go into it," Mac said through gritted teeth. "Or I'll make you dive into that snow and fish out the cigar using only your teeth."

Tim stepped back, chuckled. "What's with the violence?" He was trying to be funny, and although the clown act had worked on their frat brothers in college, it was going nowhere tonight. When Tim realized that Mac was having none of his BS, he shrugged his shoulders. "Oh, hell. Fine. It was a long time ago, junior year. I'd just finished soccer practice and I was getting a few things out of my locker. I heard a girl and a guy in an empty classroom. It was late, after five." He shrugged again. "I thought it was a couple of kids fooling around and I was going to jump out and scare the crap out of them." Mac raised his eyebrows. "It wasn't a couple of kids. It was Olivia."

"And?"

"And the math teacher."

Mac cursed.

"Yep."

"So, you didn't jump out?"

"Hell no!"

Mac could see why Olivia felt embarrassed about something like that. But hell, everyone did stupid things when they were kids. One question remained though. He stared hard at Tim. "I don't get it. Why is she so angry at you?"

Tim blew out a breath. "I didn't exactly keep the news to myself."

Anger smashed through Mac like a tidal wave. "What? You told someone about what you'd seen?"

"A few people actually." He quickly reacted to the hard look on Mac's face. "C'mon, it was high school. If you can't talk trash about the school skank, what fun is—"

Mac stopped him with a deadly glare. His voice low, he asked, "What did you call her?"

Swallowing hard, Tim dropped his gaze and tried to play it off with humor. "C'mon, man, it was a long time ago."

Mac stared at Tim as if he were seeing him for the first time—and he looked a like a major ass. He said evenly, "It was a long time ago, but you clearly haven't grown up one day since then. You need to leave, Keavy."

"What?"

"Right now."

"You've got to be kidding."

"Do I look like I'm kidding?"

"I don't get you, man." Tim hugged himself against the cold and swayed from foot to foot. "Why do you care about this? She's your employee, not your…" Tim stopped moving. "Holy sh—"

"Don't," Mac warned menacingly.

"You like her. Wow. I haven't seen you really get into a woman since…" He searched his memory. "I was going to say college, but you really just played around then, too."

Mac scowled. "I'm going inside now. I'll think up something to tell Avery, then you need to get the hell out of my house."

"Look, Mac," Tim started, changing his tune as he looked almost sincere, "I was a kid…"

"We're done here." Mac left his former friend in the cold and went inside.

"Door County, Wisconsin, is the sweetest spot in the Midwest. Beautiful wildlife. It's kind of a kitschy area with friendly people who don't try to get in your business—it's my kind of place. We bought some land six years ago and built our dream home." Louise sighed as she sat in front of the fireplace and sipped her buttered rum. "Traveling is fun and always a great adventure, but nothing feels better than going home, you know?"

Olivia nodded, but she didn't exactly feel that way about her two-bedroom apartment. Sure, it was pretty and bright and had a decent kitchen, but it wasn't exactly her dream home.

"When are you going back, Louise?" Avery asked, curled up like a pretty blond cat on the sofa, while Harold inspected a book on architecture that had been on the coffee table.

"Tomorrow morning. We want to be there in time to start decorating for the holidays. Harold and I have this thing for Christmas trees. We go to the lot ourselves and pick out one for every room in the house."

"Every room?" Olivia asked disbelievingly.

Louise laughed. "Yes."

"It's beautiful," Avery said knowingly. "And that pine scent everywhere…"

"You know," Louise said to both Avery and Olivia, "we're having all of Harold's family for Christmas." She lowered her voice. "He has an enormous and very judgmental family."

"I can hear you, honey," Harold said, flipping through the pages of his book. "I'm sitting right here."

With an impish smile she continued, "They have always taunted me about not being able to cook and take care of my man, so this year I have vowed to create the best Thanksgiving dinner anyone has ever seen." She paled. "I have no idea how I'm going to manage it though. Unlike you, Olivia, I have zero skill."

"It's not that difficult," Olivia assured her, trying to be as supportive as she could. Anyone could learn to cook, but in her opinion Thanksgiving dinner was not the best place to start. "The simpler the better. All you need are a few recipes."

"A few?" Louise repeated nervously.

Olivia laughed. "Before you go in the morning, I could give you a little lesson in—"

Suddenly, Louise's face brightened, her eyes rounded and she burst out, "That's a wonderful idea."

"Great," Olivia said. "So, meet me in the kitchen say around—"

"No. That's not what I mean."

Confused, Olivia shook her head. "I'm sorry…I don't understand."

Louise grinned widely. "You're done working for Mac tomorrow, right?"

"Yes."

"Then come with us to Door County."

"What?"

Louise looked beyond excited, like a kid, sitting forward in her seat. She put her mug on the coffee table. "Stay for a few days and teach me how to cook. In style, too—the kitchen is awesome, and I have every tool…every tool I have no idea how to use."

Still in shock, Olivia just muttered, "Wow. I don't know."

This time, Harold jumped in. "Why not? You travel for your job, right?"

"Right, but—"

Louise laughed. "I know I'm not a bachelor looking for help, but couldn't you extend your client base to include clueless, helpless females, too?"

Olivia glanced from Harold to Avery to Louise. They were all smiling. Why couldn't she do this? She was done with Mac, and she'd love to see Door County and help the DeBolds. She shrugged and smiled herself. "Okay. I'll have to check my schedule, see if I've been booked. But if not, I'm all yours."

"Great." Clasping her hands together, Louise turned

to her husband and hooted. "I'm going to wipe those evil, know-it-all smirks off your family's faces."

Harold's lips twitched. "They don't smirk, darling."

It was at that moment that Mac entered the room. He spotted Avery and gave her a terse glance. "Avery, your husband's not feeling well. You'd better take him home."

Avery looked concerned. "What?"

"Tim needs to go."

A small flicker of concern tapped at Olivia's insides. What had gone down between the two of them to make Mac look so annoyed and Tim rush out? What was said? Her heart dipped as she wondered what Tim had revealed.

"He's waiting for you by the front door," Mac told Avery brusquely.

"Oh. Okay." Slightly confused, Avery stood and offered a quick goodbye to Olivia and the DeBolds before leaving the room.

Without another word about it, Mac turned his attention to the threesome remaining. His eyes were cool and detached, but he was forcing a grin. "You all look excited about something."

"Is Tim all right?" Olivia asked.

"He'll be fine," Mac stated quickly and without an ounce of emotion.

Louise looked serious for a moment. "I hope so."

Mac nodded, then glanced around expectantly. "So, what did I miss?"

Louise didn't hesitate to switch topics, "We're talking about Harold's family and how they're going to drop their jaws when I cook and serve them Thanksgiving dinner."

"Looks as though my wife has hired Olivia to teach her how to cook," Harold informed him on a chuckle.

"Really?" He looked at Olivia, his jaw set.

"Could be. If I'm free." He didn't look pleased, but Olivia couldn't tell exactly what was going on behind his eyes. Was it whatever had happened with Tim or the prospect of Olivia working for the DeBolds that had him fuming?

"Where are you going?"

"To our home in Wisconsin," Louise said, but Mac was still staring at Olivia.

"When?"

"Tomorrow."

"No." Mac said the word so darkly and succinctly that everyone stopped and stared at him.

"What's wrong?" Olivia asked Mac.

Mac recovered quickly, his tone now ultraprofessional as he addressed her. "You and I haven't finished our business yet."

"Huh?"

Harold and Louise exchanged glances, and Harold cleared his throat. "I'm sorry, Mac. We didn't know."

It was then that Mac realized he was about to alienate the clients he wanted so badly to score. "No, no," he said, chuckling, back in total control now. "I'm the one who's sorry. My business is so all-consuming these days, I didn't get a chance to ask Olivia to continue on."

"All-consuming," Harold repeated with understanding. "Well, that's why we agreed to come here, isn't it?

And why we're considering transferring our financial holdings to you."

"Well," Mac began, "my new project with Olivia doesn't have to start immediately. But I would like a chance to talk with you both, show you the plans I have created for your future. Do you have room for one more in Door County…?"

Harold seemed to like this idea and nodded in agreement. "Kill two birds, is that it?"

Mac nodded.

Olivia sat on the floor fuming. She did not appreciate Mac's interference or his interloping ways, but before she could even get a word out, Harold was talking again—sounding pumped up and making specific plans.

"Okay," he said. "So while the women are in the kitchen—"

"Hey, watch yourself, Harold," Louise warned good-naturedly, going to sit beside him on the couch. "Make sure you don't add a 'where they belong' to the end of that sentence."

He patted her leg. "Never, darling." Then he turned back to Mac. "While the women are in the kitchen plotting against my family, you and I can do some ice fishing and talk about how you're going to make us richer than we already are."

"Richer, more secure and totally protected."

Harold beamed. "I like the sound of that."

Olivia knew she had zero control over her immediate future. The DeBolds had found a perfect situation, and as they sat there grinning they had that rich person's, "we're going to make it happen no matter what anyone says" look on their faces.

Olivia stood and started gathering plates and cups, knowing full well that Mac was watching her, feeling like he'd won, like he had more time to get her into bed. She swallowed thickly at the thought, trying to ignore the pounding of her heart.

The only thing that could save her now was if her partners had booked another job for her.

Thirteen

All the excited chatter about Mary's upcoming engagement party came to a screeching halt when Olivia walked into No Ring Required's modern kitchen and announced her plans to fly to Door County the following day. Seated at the table, Tess and Mary listened intently as Olivia explained that she was going to Wisconsin to teach Louise DeBold how to cook Thanksgiving dinner, and that Mac Valentine was going along, as well.

Mary cupped her mug of tea and tried to be the rational one. "Okay, I personally think it's great that we're expanding to include women who don't have, or who choose not to grow, the stereotypical 'wifely' gene, it's just…" Her voice trailed off.

"I'll finish for her," Tess stated boldly, pulling her red

hair into a loose bun. "The fact that your former client, Mac Valentine, is going with you is a little bizarre."

Olivia sat beside Mary. "I know, but Harold DeBold wants to get to know him better and hear his plans for their financial future before he'll give Mac his business. So, you see, it's really two separate gigs going on here."

"Uh-huh," was all Tess said.

"Going out of town seems to be where trouble starts," Mary said, touching her belly.

Olivia frowned at her. "You don't consider little Ethan or Ethanette here trouble, do you?"

"No, of course not. I just mean, when you're out of town you're not in your comfort zone and you look to someone else for comfort—that is, if you're attracted to that someone else." She leaned forward. "Are you? Are you attracted to that someone else?"

"I refuse to answer on the grounds that this one—" she pointed behind her to a looming Tess "—might sucker punch me, or something."

Tess laid a hand on Olivia's shoulder and said sweetly, "I'm fair. I'd at least have you turn around before I hit you."

Mary laughed, and Olivia grimaced. "This is partly your fault, ladies."

"How is it our fault?" Tess demanded, sitting across from them.

"Maybe someone should've booked me for another gig starting today."

Tess snorted. "Maybe you need to stand up to this guy and tell him to take a hike."

"Maybe I will." Both women looked unconvinced, and Olivia sighed with frustration. "Look, you two, the only comfort I'll be cooking up is in the kitchen, okay?"

Tess and Mary continued to vocalize their opinions and concerns for the rest of the day. Then later, when Olivia returned home to pack, the phone call to her father didn't go much better....

"You are insane to go anywhere with that man," said Owen Winston angrily.

She had him on speakerphone, and was packing a suitcase while they talked. "Dad, I didn't call for advice, I called to let you know that I was going to be out of town for a few days."

"To the diamond DeBolds house in Door County." He made a noise that sounded awfully like an out-of-tune French horn. "Door County is a place for couples on vacation. Did you know that?"

Yes, she did, and it probably worried her more than it did him, but she wasn't about to let her father know that. "Will you go by my apartment and feed my fish...once a day? Will you?"

He heaved a sigh. "Of course. We don't want them to suffer."

She laughed at his sarcasm. "Will it hurt your masculine pride if I tell you that you're acting like a drama queen?"

"Livy, tell me you're not falling for that bastard."

She stopped packing. "No falling."

"Good. And tell me you're not going to—"

"Stop. Dad. Please don't go there." This was it.

Maybe this was it. The opportunity for her to tell her father the truth. Not the details, but the basics of what she'd done in high school, so that if Mac ever did approach her father with the information it wouldn't come as a shock.

"I'm sorry, Livy," he said, sounding sad and maybe a little lonely. "I love you and I just want…"

"The best for me, I know—I get it." She bit her lip, thought about how to say it, how to begin…then she remembered how Mac had promised not to use her past against her by going to her father, and she found an excuse to leave it alone, or at the very least, put it off until maybe she and her father were face-to-face.

She tossed a few sweaters into her suitcase and said, "I love you, Dad, and I'll see you on Thursday."

Fourteen

Mac enjoyed the solitude of a private plane. He had a rule: if he was going to be in the air for more than an hour, he always chartered a Gulfstream. He glanced around with an assessing gaze. The DeBolds' Citation was smaller than what he was used to, but comfortable enough once he was seated. He was curious to see how it felt once they got it in the air, as eight-seaters could act a little unsteady at times. The interior was ultraplush, though, outfitted with soft leather and thick carpet, and the very capable steward, Tom, had set out glasses and a bottle of sparkling water.

Just outside the plane Mac heard Tom greet another passenger. Mac glanced up from his laptop, annoyed at the jolt of excitement that ran through him when Olivia Winston came aboard.

"Morning," Mac said.

She gave him a friendly smile. "Hey." She took the single seat across the aisle from him. "Are we early?"

"I don't think so."

His gaze moved over her, from the soft chocolate-brown sweater to the jeans that stretched temptingly over her thighs and hips when she sat. His hands itched to touch her. It had been too long and he could hardly wait to have her—in his arms and in his bed. Up until this point, there had been too many distractions, and he'd been unsuccessful in his attempts to seduce her. Now that they were going away together…

The steward came out and addressed them, his large blue eyes and round face filled with practiced friendliness. "Welcome aboard, Ms. Winston, Mr. Valentine."

"Thank you," Olivia said warmly.

"Is there anything I can get you?"

"Not for me, thanks." She turned to Mac. "Anything you need, Valentine?"

He grinned at her and uttered, "Nothing that Tom can provide."

She rolled her eyes at him, then glanced back at the steward. "We're fine, thank you."

He nodded. "We'll be leaving in just a few minutes. Please fasten your seat belts."

Tom was about to head for the cockpit when Olivia called out, "Excuse me."

"Yes, Miss Winston?"

"Aren't we missing a few passengers?"

The steward looked confused and just a tad annoyed. "I'm sorry?"

"The DeBolds?"

"Oh, no, miss. They went home last night, and sent the plane and myself back for the two of you."

Olivia looked at Mac, then back at Tom. "Why?"

"I don't know, miss."

The man stood there. And Mac, growing tired of both Tom's put-out attitude and Olivia's questions, decided to step in. Sitting on the tarmac wasn't his idea of a good time. "Thank you, Tom. Now, let's get this lady in the air, shall we."

Looking relieved, the man nodded. "I'll inform the captain."

When he was gone, Olivia turned to Mac, her dark eyebrows drawn together in a frown. "Why wouldn't they call us, have us all leave together?"

Mac shrugged. "Why does it matter?"

"I'm just curious. It's a little odd."

Below their feet, the engine sprang to life with an easy vibration.

"I have a feeling they're trying to get us together," Olivia remarked, fastening her seat belt.

"We are together."

"You know what I mean, Mac."

"Ah, yes." He grinned at her over his laptop. "And what if they are? Would that be so wrong?"

She glared at him. "What is it with married people?

Why do they always feel like they need to make more couples?"

"Maybe they want others to experience their blissful state."

"Do you really believe that, Valentine?"

"Nope."

She laughed. She had a great laugh, throaty and youthful, and he had an incredible desire to always keep her laughing, keep her happy.

"Listen, Valentine, I think we need to try and remember why we're here." She was leaning back in her seat, her head tilted toward him.

"And why are we here…?"

"To work," she said, humor dancing in her eyes. "Or in your case, to work and exact revenge on my father through poor little me."

He couldn't help it—he smiled at her, and she returned it. She was something else, no wilting flower. Why did it excite him that she understood exactly what he was after and wasn't afraid to take him on?

"Speaking of revenge…" she began, her eyes suddenly not meeting his.

"Yes?"

"Did your friend give you any helpful ammunition the other night?"

Mac's jaw tightened. "No."

She was quiet for a moment, then said, "Tim didn't tell you about…what happened?"

He stared at her, hard and intense. "Listen, Olivia, I told you before, I don't care what happened in your past. I don't need to use BS hearsay from a former friend to get what I want from you."

"Former friend?"

"I'm not sentimental. I don't value friendships. And if someone crosses me, goes too far, I have no problem walking away."

She nodded. "I'll remember that."

A slow grin moved over his lips. "Now, let's get back to talking about why we're here."

"Right. To work."

Mac sighed. "I'd hoped you'd forgotten."

She laughed. "Nope. And odds are Louise and Harold are going to throw more of this—" she gestured around the interior of the cabin "—our way."

"More private planes, more romantic destinations...sounds like hell on earth."

"You don't want to take any of this seriously."

"No."

She sighed and looked away. "Well, I do. And if you have any sense you'll focus on landing this client, not getting me into bed."

Damn, he liked her—he liked her attitude, her spirit, her brains, the way she moved and how her eyes always spoke for her. But there was no way he was going to allow his feelings to interfere with the facts. He wanted payback. Of course he wasn't about to use her past or Tim's account of it against her. He would only work with what he had now—his desire for her, and to take Owen's daughter to his bed. Mac would have what he wanted: revenge and a woman he desired above all things.

The plane backed up slowly, getting in position to taxi. "Not to worry, Olivia," he said with a tone of arrogant confidence. "I'm fully capable of landing both you and the DeBolds."

Comprised of a sprawling log house, orchard and barn, the DeBolds' home was truly one of the most unique places Olivia had ever seen and she was completely enchanted by it. On fifty private acres, just a half mile north of Sturgeon Bay, the custom log home was already being dressed for the holidays. When Mac and Olivia arrived, a crew of ten or so men and women were working outside, affixing garlands, wreaths and twinkle lights to trees, doors, rooftops and anything else that didn't move.

Olivia gave a low whistle as she stepped out of the Town Car that had picked them up from the airport. "Okay, I grew up in a very nice house with very nice furnishings—most of which you couldn't touch—but this…this is spectacular."

Mac helped the driver with their luggage, told the guy that he could handle it from there, then gave him a hefty tip.

As the car pulled away, Olivia stood in the driveway and just stared at the house, transfixed. "I wouldn't think that anything so big could feel so warm and friendly, but it does." She leaned down and picked up her small carry-on, as Mac had the rest of the luggage. "I think I know where I'm retiring to."

"Really?" Mac said, sounding surprised.

"Yes, really." She followed him up the walk to the front door. "This is my fantasy home. If they have horses, I'm just going to tie myself to one of the fence posts and cry squatter's rights."

"I don't get it. I mean, it's 'cute' in a country bumpkin sort of way, but—"

"Yeah, I know it's not like that glass and stainless steel penthouse of yours in Manhattan, but—"

He stopped, shot her a sideways glance. "How did you know about my apartment in Manhattan?"

"Oh, Mac," she said on a laugh, "you never stop underestimating me. Great place, by the way, very James Bond meets Times Square."

"Thanks," he muttered as they reached the front door. "I think."

"But this place is way cooler. What could you possibly not like here?"

"It's just a little too much like a bed-and-breakfast," he said, dropping the bags onto the DeBolds' massive monogrammed welcome mat.

She snorted. "You're such a guy."

Before she could stop him, Mac snaked a hand around her waist and pulled her close. "Damn right."

Olivia gasped, and even though it was twenty degrees outside, heat accosted her skin like a blast from an oven.

"But, hey," he said gently, gazing down at her, "if you like this place, that's all that matters. I'm more than willing to accept patchwork quilts, sunflower wallpaper and rasp-berry-colored bathrooms if you'll share it with me."

The soft, sweet way he was looking at her made

Olivia almost believe him. And yet she chose sarcasm over sincerity. "Interesting. Sounds like you've been to a B and B a few times before. You've got the description of every bed-and-breakfast I've ever heard about down pat."

"I've been sent to a few Web sites in my time."

"By a few ladies?" His lips were so close, looked so good—and she could remember exactly how they felt.

"Women seem to think 'homespun' is romantic."

"And it's not?"

He slowly shook his head. "Not to me."

Power pulsed from him, strength and sexuality, too. It was a hard combination to resist. And again, she questioned herself, questioned why she needed to resist at all. Why couldn't she just have fun here and not hold back? She was an adult, maybe a foolish one, but hey…

"I'll probably kick myself later for asking this," she said, "but what is romantic to you?"

"Well, this doesn't suck." He grinned mischievously, then glanced up.

Olivia followed his gaze and spotted a sprig of mistletoe hanging from a beam over the porch. "Now this is just awkward," she began, laughing. "What if the mail carrier and the UPS guy got here at the same time—"

"Ah, shut up, Winston." He cut her off with a growl, then covered her mouth with his. His nose was cold, but his lips seared with heat and need, and Olivia melted into his embrace.

"You smell good," he whispered against her lips.

"It's the snow."

"No."

"Pine trees."

"No," he said, applying soft kisses first to her top lip then to the bottom one. "It's you."

Her breath caught in her throat as he kissed her again, hot, sweet kisses that made her forget where she was. Like a blind woman, searching, hungry, she slipped her hands inside his coat and ran her fingers over his trim waist to his back, then upward. The muscles in his shoulders flexed, and she gripped at them, squeezed at them as she tipped her chin up to get closer. She just wanted to get closer to him.

It was at that moment the front door opened. Like a guilty child with both of her hands stuck in the forbidden cookie jar, Olivia jumped away from Mac.

Pulling the door wide, Louise looked from Olivia to Mac, just a touch of confusion on her perfectly made-up face. "Did you ring the bell? We didn't hear anything."

Olivia quickly said, "We…just arrived." She looked at Mac to corroborate this, but he only stared at her, his eyes rife with amusement. Of course he wasn't going to be any help.

A broad grin on her face, Louise said, "That's odd. One of the decorators came inside to tell me you were here."

Which meant that said meddlesome decorator probably also mentioned what Mac and Olivia were doing out on the porch.

As Louise ushered them inside, Olivia muttered a terse, "Oh, man," back at Mac, which only made him chuckle.

"Harold," Louise called up a beautiful log staircase. "They're here." Then she turned back to Mac and Olivia. "Have a good flight?"

Trying to brush off any residual embarrassment, Olivia forced a smile. "It was great, thank you."

They followed Louise into a massive, two-level great room with hardwood floors, exposed beams and a rock fireplace that stretched all the way to the cathedral ceiling. The open floor plan was spectacular, allowing visitors to see the living room, dining area and huge chef's kitchen, with a rectangular black granite island, from the entryway.

"You have an amazing home," Olivia remarked. "I'm completely in love with it, and this area."

Louise beamed. "Well then, you'll have to get out of the kitchen while you're here and experience Door County fully—or our property, at the very least. We have horses and orchards, and cross-country skiing is a blast."

From beside her, Mac touched the small of her back. "Horses, Olivia."

"Yes, I heard. Very exciting," Olivia said, stepping away from him so her cheeks—and several other parts of her—wouldn't go up in flames from his touch.

Above them, a creaking sound echoed on the landing, and a few seconds later, Harold trotted down the stairs. He had a big grin on his face when he saw them. "Welcome, welcome," he said warmly, shaking Mac's hand, then Olivia's. "Good to have you both here."

"We're looking forward to the stay," Mac said. "Great place you have here."

Olivia shot him a look as Harold said, "Thank you."

"So, I suppose you both would you like to get settled before lunch?" Louise asked

"I'm a big unpacker," Olivia joked. "So, that would be great."

Harold looked at Louise, who looked at him with big eyes, then she turned to Mac and Olivia. "We wanted to have you stay in the house, but we're having the rooms fixed up for Harold's family, and of course they're very particular about what they want."

"Easy, honey," Harold said on a chuckle.

"Anyway, we have two small guest houses on the property, and we've had them made up for you."

"Guest houses?" Olivia said, feeling a little worried. Guest houses were a little like hotel suites. Staying in the house was far safer. "Are you sure we're not putting you out?"

Louise laughed as though this were the silliest idea she'd ever heard. "I'm going to get lunch ready. Not to torment you, but so you'll be able to see my skill level—or lack thereof—and Johnny, our groundskeeper, will take you across the pond to the guest houses."

Across the pond. Right.

Those guest houses had better be a good fifty yards away from each other, she mused as Harold called for Johnny over the intercom. It took no more than thirty seconds for the tall young man to show up, an easy smile on his thin face.

After thanking the DeBolds for their hospitality again, Mac and Olivia followed Johnny down a long flagstone path and around a small pond, which was tree-lined and frozen solid.

When Olivia saw the adjoining guest houses, her heart leaped into her throat. They were too close, only separated by a wall, for goodness' sake. But when they were ushered inside the first house, her heart sank. Decorated from top to bottom in luxurious whites and creams, soft rugs and warm lighting, Olivia knew she was in trouble. The large one-room suite screamed romance, from the small fir tree, which was dressed in white lights, to the massive stone fireplace, to the four-poster, king-sized bed with down pillows and terrycloth robe draped across the comforter, to the double whirl-pool tub not ten feet away.

Olivia put her hands on her hips and sighed. "Oh, yeah, they're trying to hook us up."

Beside her, Mac chuckled. "Want to come and see my room? Maybe it looks even more like a room at a bed-and-breakfast than yours does."

She didn't think that was possible, and she uttered, "Some other time."

"Promise?"

When she glanced up at him, saw the wicked gleam in his dark eyes and the curl of a smile on his extraordinarily handsome face, she felt her knees grow weak and knew it was only a matter of time before the rest of her followed suit. Because seriously, how much could a girl resist?

Fifteen

"I'm really sorry about lunch. I was trying to impress you, and I ended up almost killing you."

If someone were looking at Louise DeBold from the outside they'd see a confident, beautiful, sharp woman who owned every room she walked into and didn't need accolades from anyone to feel her value. But as she stood in front of Olivia, a semicooked turkey sitting on a platter of greens, she looked as though she'd shrunk in both stature and self-confidence.

Olivia took the platter from her and set it on the island. "You didn't know the turkey was undercooked."

"I would if I'd have cut into it."

Olivia laughed. "True."

Ripping off her apron, Louise sighed. "I think I might be hopeless."

"You're not."

"Harold's family is going to have a field day with this." She sat at the island. "I don't fail at things, Olivia, you know? I was an appraiser for ten years—the top gemologist in the country. Everyone came to me…." She stared at the turkey as though she'd just gone to war with it and had come back bruised and defeated. "I can't fail at this."

"You won't," Olivia assured her. "Now, get that apron back on and come over to the cutting board. We're going to try this again."

"All right."

"Poultry is a tricky thing," Olivia explained as she took another small bird out of the fridge and laid it in the sink. "I like to compare it to a relationship."

At this Louise perked up. "How so?"

"If it's not seasoned right or given enough heat, it will fail. Not to mention become boring and bland."

"Wow."

"That's right," Olivia said as she pulled out the bag of giblets and other delicious innards from inside the turkey. Then she washed it inside and out and patted it dry with paper towels.

"So," Louise began tentatively, "if I may be so bold as to ask, are you and Mac good poultry or bad poultry?"

Olivia took a second before answering to assess the warming feeling that had seeped into her belly. "We don't have a relationship."

"So, earlier on the porch…"

"Was a moment of insanity."

Louise sighed. "God, I love those."

Olivia laughed, she couldn't help herself. "Mac and me…it's complicated."

"Uncomplicate it, then—just like you're doing for me with this damn bird. Dress it, season it well, stick it in the oven on the right temp and baste, baste, baste."

Olivia pointed at her. "You've got this down, Louise."

"I like you, both of you," she said, seasoning the inside of the turkey with salt and pepper. "It would be fun to do this again."

"It would, but it might be a separate thing. While Mac is an amazing money man, he wants nothing to do with relationships."

"You never know, Liv." She paused, looked up. "Can I call you that?"

Olivia smiled. "Of course."

"Harold was a total player when we met," Louise said as she dug under the skin, loosening it from the breast.

"Really?"

"Uh-huh."

"I can't imagine it."

She stuffed the breast with sprigs of sage and thyme. "Well, it's true. Different chick every night. And look at him now." She slathered the top of the bird with butter. "Today, he brought home all this beautiful wood. He wants to build a baby crib, all by himself."

"Baby crib—are you…"

She smiled as she walked over to the sink to rinse her

hands. "My point is, you just never know what people are capable of until you give them the chance. Now, let's put this thing in the oven and get to work on the stuffing."

When Mac walked into the kitchen two hours later, Harold in his wake, the scent of Thanksgiving nearly bowled him over. He spotted Olivia at the sink with Louise, watching over the diamond queen as she carefully poured steaming boiled potatoes into a stainless mesh bowl. They looked very cozy, the two of them, almost like friends.

Harold elbowed him in the ribs and whispered, "I know it may be sexist, but look at our girls, wearing aprons and cooking their men some supper. Almost makes a guy want to grunt and scratch himself."

Chuckling softly, Mac said, "Almost." But he was hardly laughing inside. His reaction to Harold's comment worried him. *Our girls*—the phrase should've washed over him, meant nothing, hell, meant less than nothing. But the idea of Olivia belonging to him in any real, meaningful way made his heart ache strangely.

Now, as a kid he'd been put in and taken out of home after home until he was close to fourteen. Thanksgiving and family really hadn't meant anything sacred or special. So maybe it was that when he looked at Olivia with Louise in the kitchen, being all domestic and looking content—and with the smells of a happy home curling through his nostrils—it had triggered something. Something he might want at some point in his life.

At some point, but not now...

"I love this part," Louise was saying as she smashed the hot potatoes with something that looked like a branding iron. "Gets out all your aggressions."

They hadn't noticed Mac and Harold yet.

"Don't I know it." Laughing, Olivia poured the hot cranberry relish into a bowl. "The key to good cooking is to make simple food with really fresh ingredients."

"Something smells good in here," Harold said, walking past Mac and slipping his arms around his wife's waist as she continued to beat the potatoes into submission.

Glancing over her shoulder, Louise smiled. "Yes, a proper lunch. Even if it is two o'clock."

Mac looked over at Olivia. She was watching the happy couple, her eyes melancholy. Then she noticed him looking at her and offered him a gentle smile. Mac's body stirred. What would happen if he walked over and put his arms around her, kissed her neck as she stirred sugar into those plumped-up cranberries? Would she want to get lost in the fantasy that the DeBolds had created and were slowly but surely sucking them into?

"So, did you two have an interesting talk?" Louise asked Harold and Mac.

"Interesting doesn't begin to cover it," Harold said, releasing Louise from his grasp. "This guy is too damn smart. Why Avery didn't introduce us sooner, I'll never know. The amount we could've been saving in taxes…" He shook his head.

"So do we have a new financial advisor then?" Louise asked.

"It would seem that way."

Olivia glanced at Mac, gave him a tight-lipped smile. It could've been congratulatory or sad, he didn't have a clue.

"We'll have to give Avery a call," Louise said, "and have her draw up the papers."

Harold nodded. "Right."

Mac's jaw clenched at the mention of Avery. He hadn't spoken to either her or Tim since he'd tossed the latter out of his house the other night. He'd have to work out his relationship with Avery, but he was done with her husband. Mac glanced up and saw Olivia watching him, curious. He forced his mood to lighten and winked at her. Then he addressed Harold.

"Not so fast," he said, joking with Harold. "You know I'm only taking you on as a client if you can play a serious game of pool."

Harold raised his brows at his wife. "Can you spare me for a few hours after dinner?"

"You've been challenged, honey," she said. "I don't see how you can't go." She held up her bowl of potatoes. "But right now, you're going to sit at the table, eat the meal we've prepared and then promptly tell me what an amazing cook I am."

"Done." Harold growled, kissed her neck. "Then after lunch, I want you to lie down for a while, okay?"

"What about our guests?"

"We're fine." Olivia carried stuffing and cranberries to the long pine table. "I have a book and Mac always has work to—"

"No way," Louise said severely, her dark eyes narrowed. "Didn't you say you loved horses, Olivia?"

Mac took a basket of rolls from Olivia's hands and nodded before heading to the table. "Yes, she did."

"Perfect. The horses need some exercise." As if she had just solved an enormous problem, Louise smiled contently and they all sat down at the table and marveled at the delicious-looking pre-Thanksgiving feast. "A ride in the Door County snow is a must-do for every couple."

Olivia's head came up with a jerk. "Louise…"

"I meant, every*one*." But the giggle that followed completely and obviously negated her quick correction.

They weren't a couple, but as far as Olivia was concerned there was nothing more romantic than horseback riding through the snow with Mac, dipping under naked, brittle branches, galloping across an open field iced with white. For the first time since they'd arrived, Olivia understood what Mary had meant about the dangers of getting out of her element, her comfort zone, and hanging around with a guy she could see herself kissing until she was both sweaty and naked.

As she slowed her chestnut mare to a brisk walk, Olivia breathed in the cold air. She turned to look at Mac. He was like something out of the movie *Camelot,* in a modern wool coat and scarf, of course, but he had rugged, thick dark hair, and that one-with-the-horse thing going on, and she didn't even try and stop herself from imagining him sitting in front of her, her arms wrapped around his waist as they gave the mare some serious exercise.

The sky was starting to lose its afternoon warmth when Olivia stopped in the middle of a snowy field and took in the faded colors of the sunset. "Come on, Valentine, tell me this doesn't beat the Manhattan skyline by a mile."

His horse, a proud gray palomino, was a little frisky and Mac had to circle him around Olivia and her horse a few times to get him to calm down. "I don't know," he began. "What's so amazing? Fifty acres of trees, natural springs and killer views. I don't get it."

She laughed at his lighthearted sarcasm. "So, are you headed home tomorrow?"

"What?"

Their horses puffed out warm breath into the cold air. "You bagged the DeBolds. It's a done deal. Harold as much as said he was ready to sign on the X when we were at lunch."

"He was ready to sign back in Minneapolis."

"What?" Olivia said, confused, studying him.

A hint of a smile curved his lips. "Harold and Louise would've signed papers before they left Minneapolis if I had pushed for it."

"Then why didn't you?"

He chuckled. "C'mon, Liv. You know why I'm really here."

Catching the spark of challenge in his eyes, Olivia took a shivering breath. "You have a huge new client, and you said that one of your former clients has come back. Do you really still feel the need for payback?"

He regarded her with amused impatience. "I feel the need for you. The payback is just a bonus."

His unguarded, hungry look sent chills running through her body. Saying nothing, she turned her horse around and headed back toward the barn. With a click of his tongue, Mac spurred his horse forward to catch up with her.

When they were riding side by side again, he said, "I know you're as curious as I am."

"About what?"

"What my skin would feel like against yours."

"Mac…c'mon…"

But he wouldn't stop. "How long you could hold out before you begged me to kiss you somewhere other than your mouth. What it would feel like when I pushed inside of you, climaxed with you."

His words went straight to the core of her, and she swallowed against the tightness in her throat. She was in trouble here or she was about to allow herself a good time…she wasn't sure which. "I am curious, but I'd hoped I could hold out." She saw the gentle slope of the barn up ahead, looking like a wood-hewn salvation. She forced herself to look at him, into those dark, wicked eyes. "Honestly, I'm not so sure I can hold out—or want to anymore."

A flush that had nothing to do with the cold crossed his cheeks. "Well, that's an admission."

"Yeah."

They rode back to the barn in silence. Around them, the air swirled with new, fresh snow, and the sky grew gray as afternoon came to a close. Inside the stables, Johnny was nowhere in sight, and after climbing down and tying up his horse, Mac reached for Olivia, helping her off her horse and onto her feet.

"I'm going back to the room to take a shower before dinner," Olivia said quietly, trying to disentangle herself from his grasp.

But Mac held her firm.

She looked up at him. "What are you doing?"

"Holding you until you stop fighting."

Running on instinct, Olivia tried to push away from him, get free of the rousing feel of his body against hers. But it was no use. She growled her frustration. She wanted him. There was no more denying it, to herself or to him. Damn it, why should she have to deny herself? Sure it might be a mistake, he might be a mistake, but so what? She was old enough now to deal with her stupid choices.

She stared at his mouth, that full, hard mouth that could crush her with his words, yet make her want nothing more than to leave all past mistakes and promises in the dust. "What are you waiting for then?"

His hot gaze swept her, but he said nothing.

She laughed out of sheer insanity. "Kiss me, damn it!"

He laughed, too. But he quickly sobered, let his head fall forward against hers. "Olivia, understand that if I kiss you now, I'm not going to be able to stop."

"I don't want you to."

"And I want you more than I've ever wanted anything in my life." He pulled her against him and gave her a deep, all-consuming kiss on the mouth.

Olivia could barely breathe when he released her, grabbed her hand and uttered hoarsely, "Come with me."

Leaving the horses tied up, Mac led her down the center aisle of the stable, all the way to the end, then off to the right, down another corridor. When he spotted an empty stall, he pulled her inside and closed the door.

Clean, sweet-smelling hay blanketed the floor, but Olivia barely registered the fact as Mac pulled off her coat and took her in his arms. His kiss began soft and slow, light pressure on her lips as he swayed back and forth to music she couldn't hear. Then the pressure increased until she opened for him, gave him access to her tongue, until she murmured "so good" and other ridiculous utterances, until she wrapped her arms around his neck and kissed him back so intensely she felt as though she were drowning.

He left her mouth and dipped his head, nuzzling her neck, nibbling at the thin flesh over her pulse, making her blood race in her veins. It had been so long, and she couldn't wait to feel his skin on her skin, the weight of him as he pressed into her. Just the thought of having him inside her had her feeling weak and hot and wet.

Somehow Mac got Olivia onto her back, but the change of position barely registered. All she knew was that one moment she was standing, and the next, her body was cradled in a soft nest of hay.

"What if someone comes…?" she uttered breathlessly. "Sees us…"

Positioned above her, Mac unbuttoned her shirt. "I don't give a damn if anyone sees us."

She refused to recall the last time someone had seen

her with a man. This was different. This was right now. It was almost as if she needed to do this—this way— and she felt no shame in her actions.

His hands found her belly, and she sucked air between her teeth at the sheer pleasure of him touching her naked skin, so close to the center of her, where she ached. She wanted him to just get to it, send his hand lower and put her out of her misery. Hell, she was already so worked up it would only take ten seconds— maybe less.

But Mac wasn't going there, not yet.

She wore a bra that clasped in the front and he easily took care of it, casting aside the two pale pink wisps of fabric. The fading light of afternoon filtered through the small square window above them, and Mac looked down at her and shook his head. "You have no idea…"

"What?"

"How long I've wanted to see you like this, and touch you. And now, I feel like I should take time to just…marvel."

She laughed, but it was almost a pained sound. "You do and I'll kill you."

He gave a quick, husky laugh, then bent his head and dragged his mouth over one of her breasts, then the other, applying soft, irritatingly slow kisses over the skin around her nipple.

Feeling as though she was about to explode, Olivia reached up and threaded her fingers in his hair, tried to pull him down.

"Patience, Liv," he whispered, the heat of his breath sending sparks to every nerve ending.

Olivia waited, the muscles in her legs contracting, her toes pointing until finally she felt him, felt that electrifying sensation of hot, wet tongue against her hard, sensitive nipple. Her breath came out in a rush and she thrust her hips in the air. Sensing the urgency in her body, Mac lapped at the hard peak, finding a rhythm, groaning when he heard her moan as his free hand moved down…down her belly, over her hips and under the slip of cotton.

"No," he uttered hoarsely, his fingers burrowing between her thighs. "Olivia, you're too hot, and way too wet. I don't know how long I can wait."

"And you wanted me to be patient," she uttered.

He found the entrance to her body and thrust his middle finger inside of her. It was too much. She sucked in air, shivered and bucked against his hand. She almost didn't know what to do. Her hands fisted hay, and the way he was moving inside her, pressing against that deep, sensitive part of her, she felt tears drop onto her cheeks, down to her neck.

"What is it?" he whispered, concerned. "Does this hurt?"

"No," she uttered. "No. It's wonderful."

He kissed her cheek, her lips, her neck.

"Make love to me, Mac. Please. Now." She couldn't control her body and all she wanted was him, inside of her. She clawed at his shirt, tore a few buttons and unhooked the others, then pulled it off of his chest. He was so beautiful, the way the thick muscles of his chest rose and fell with each breath he took. With greedy hands, she found his zipper and tugged.

"Olivia, wait."

She shook her head, annoyed. "No. For what?"

"I don't have anything—not here."

"No.…" Her heart sank, and her mind raced for a solution. "Can't you just let me feel you, for a moment?"

"I think I only have a moment in me," he said hoarsely. "But I'll protect you, if you want that."

She nodded, wriggling out of her jeans and underwear, not giving a damn about the risks. Mac, too, pulled off his remaining clothes and wasted no time, slipping his hands under her, lifting her hips and burying himself deep inside her.

Olivia saw stars, actually saw them on the back of her closed lids. For just a moment, she let the delicious feeling of Mac inside her wash over her, then as he began to pull out, she woke up from her daydream. She gripped his hips as he thrust back inside of her, opened her legs and wrapped them around his waist, rocked with him, moaning, scratching at him, knowing she had little time left and feeling simultaneously frustrated and desperate for release.

Then Mac leaned down, caught one hard nipple between his lips and suckled deeply. She lost it. Pumping furiously, she gave in to the fire and ice of her climax, crying out, whimpering as Mac bucked and thrust inside her, the sweet feeling rolling through her.

On a curse, Mac pulled out and hovered above her.

Hardly a second elapsed before Olivia reached for him, wrapped her hand around him and stroked the thick, pulsing length of him until he sucked in air, thrust against her hand and climaxed.

He dropped down beside her on the hay, breathing heavily, his brow damp, and wrapped his arms around her. They lay there in silence, both breathing heavily, both damp with sweat, watching the last lights of day fade into the early gray of evening.

Olivia wanted to stay with him, keep him against her, but she didn't know where they stood now and that made her feel uncomfortable, as though she wanted to steal away by herself and think things through. "I want to stay," she began. "But I need to help with dinner."

"I know. Listen, Olivia." In one quick, effortless movement, he rolled her on top of him and cupped her backside possessively. His eyes blazed with a sincerity she'd never witnessed before. "You have nothing to worry about from me."

Her throat tightened with emotion as she looked down at him. "Oh, I think I have a lot to worry about with you. Just not in the way that you mean."

Chuckling, he squeezed her backside. "You might be right about that." He leaned in and kissed her gently on the mouth. "To speak in your language, sweetheart, this was just an appetizer. And I fully intend to enjoy the next course and the next and the next...."

Sixteen

Men didn't normally notice table settings or flower arrangements. They were usually hungry when they sat for dinner and just wanted to fill their bellies with whatever it was that smelled so damn good.

Sounded cavemanish, but it was true.

Mac was no exception as he sat beside Olivia at the DeBolds' dinner table, his plate piled high with fettuccine Alfredo and garlic bread. He was perfectly content at that moment. "You should be very proud of yourself, Louise. This is amazing."

Across the table, Louise looked at her husband and grinned. "Thanks, but I think my teacher should get all the credit."

"No way," Olivia retorted, twirling pasta on her fork. "You did this all by yourself. I just supervised."

Harold put an arm around his wife. "All by yourself, honey?"

"She's exaggerating."

"I am not!" Olivia insisted, laughing.

Just hearing Olivia's voice made Mac's body stir and he turned and stared at her. Dressed in a pair of funky black pants and a white sweater, she looked like a sexy ski bunny. He had every intention of being with her again tonight. As he'd said, their encounter in the barn was like a warm-up for the real thing. They'd both been too worked up, unable to take their time and really enjoy each other. Tonight, however, he was going to make her climax over and over again.

Olivia was talking to Harold, her eyes bright and happy. "And she rolled out the pasta herself."

"You did?" Harold said to Louise.

Blushing, she confirmed it. "I did."

Harold kissed her cheek, then said, "We have a pasta machine?"

Louise laughed. "Yes. Who knew, right?"

In between bites of pasta, Olivia said, "Tomorrow morning, we'll work on a few breakfast dishes that will have your in-laws apologizing for ever doubting your culinary skills." She grinned widely. "Think crab cakes benedict with lemon and parsley hollandaise, eggnog French toast and pancetta—"

"Forget apologizing," Harold interrupted merrily.

"They'll want to stay here all the time with that kind of menu."

Louise blanched. "Hmm, maybe we'd better rethink the cooking thing."

Everyone laughed, then Harold said, "Too late, honey—they're going to want to be here more often anyway when...you know."

Mac watched all three of them grin and wondered what was up, what he was missing. "Are you three going to let me in on the joke?"

"No joke," Harold said, looking at his wife in a soft, sweet way. "Louise is pregnant."

"Wow, congratulations," Mac said, reaching across the table to shake Harold's hand.

The proud father-to-be actually blushed. "Thank you."

"Do you really think your family will want to be around more?" Louise asked, a worried expression crossing her face.

"Not my family," Harold clarified. "My mother."

"Oh, Lord."

"She'll be ecstatic, sweetheart."

"She'll be meddlesome."

Finished with her pasta, Olivia dabbed her mouth with her napkin. "Well, she'll be here, and from a girl who hopes to have a child someday and has no mother to get frustrated and annoyed with for visiting too often, I say, 'you're lucky.'"

The news that Olivia's mother was not in the picture didn't come as a shock to Mac. When he was gathering information on Olivia and her father, he'd seen the obituary. But hearing her talk about it, the trace of sadness in her voice, did something to him, made him feel protective. He knew what it felt like to lose a parent, and he didn't enjoy seeing her upset.

Louise was smiling sympathetically at Olivia. "I'm sorry. I had no idea. When did you lose your mother?"

"In high school."

Mac didn't know what made him do it, but he put his hand over hers under the table. It felt good, right.

"That's awful." Shaking her head, Louise looked over to her husband. "No matter how insane your mother makes me, I'm going to grin and bear it for this little one."

Harold downed the last bite of his garlic bread. "Glad to hear it, sweetheart." He turned and winked at Olivia, who smiled in return.

As the foursome chatted and ate, Olivia did the strangest and most enchanting thing. She rotated her hand under his so that they were palm to palm, and every once in a while she gave him a gentle squeeze.

Olivia pierced a freshly made popcorn kernel with a needle and pulled the yellow fluffy bit onto the string until it met with its cranberry neighbor. As the stereo belted out Judy Garland's version of "Have Yourself a Merry Little Christmas" and the fire crackled and spit, she sat on a thick, oval rug in front of the tree, trying to teach Mac how to make garland for the little Christmas tree in her suite. It wasn't easy. The guy was a financial genius and one helluva kisser, but when it came to a needle and thread, he was all thumbs.

Mac crushed the popcorn kernel as he stuck the needle into it. Cursing, he tossed the remaining bits into the fire. "This is BS."

Olivia laughed. "Come on. No swearing when Judy Garland is singing."

"Why not? I feel sad and it's a sad song."

"It's not a sad song," she corrected. "It's an emotional song."

"Same thing."

She settled back against the base of the chenille chaise and sighed. "This was kind of me and my mom's song."

He looked at her as though she'd just stuck her needle in his side. "Okay, you can't go there when we were joking around, it makes me look like a jerk."

She smiled. "You're not a jerk." Realizing what she'd just said, she made a face, then laughed. "I can't believe I'm saying that."

He raised a sardonic eyebrow at her. "You're very funny when you're melancholy."

"My mom loved a good laugh, so she'd appreciate the dark humor in this conversation."

"When did she pass away? I know you said something at dinner...."

"When I was in high school." It was amazing that the words were still so difficult to say, and Olivia felt the urge to leap up on the bed and burrow under the covers.

"So, you were...what? Sixteen?"

"Yep."

"That's tough on a teenage girl. Mom's gone and

Dad is…" He paused, cocked his head to the side. "Dad is what?"

The direction of this conversation was starting to worry her. Mac was a sharp guy and he was putting the pieces together as he watched her. Sixteen, mom's gone, girl looks for comfort… "Dad was devastated—understandably—and he couldn't manage to do much but breathe." He was staring at her, studying her. "What?"

"Owen left you to fend for yourself, didn't he?"

Her jaw tightened. "No. He was grieving."

"So were you, Olivia."

She looked away, into the fire, her throat feeling that all too familiar tightness. She didn't want him, of all people, pointing out that her father had emotionally abandoned her for a time. It wasn't his place.

"How did you grieve, Liv? How did you manage all by yourself?"

"I wasn't by myself, damn it!" she shouted hoarsely. Fine, he got it. She hadn't been alone—she hadn't allowed herself to be alone. She'd found a substitute for the missing affection from her father, and a way to push back the pain. She grabbed her garland and a cranberry. "I went a little crazy for that first year and a half. But I got back on track, okay?"

He nodded. "Okay."

"I don't want to talk about this anymore."

"Done." He gestured to the bowl. "Can I have some more of that popcorn?"

He granted her a soft smile, and she felt the tension in her muscles relax. She let her shoulders fall and she released the breath she'd been holding since their conversation had begun. "Here you go," she said, handing him the bowl.

"I'm going to try this again."

She watched him stab at the popcorn, one piece, then two, then three. She shook her head and took away the bowl of popcorn before he crushed every piece to bits. "I'm thinking that this activity might be a little too sweet for a guy like you."

"Damn right it is," he said, reaching for a cranberry instead. "But I figure the sooner we finish decorating this tree the sooner I can kiss you."

She laughed. "Smart man. So, did you do any of this kind of thing around Christmas when you were a kid?"

"Nope. Not until I was fourteen, anyway."

"What happened when you were fourteen?"

"I was taken in by a college professor and his wife. They weren't the home-and-hearth type, but we had nice, relaxed holidays."

"Not the home-and-hearth type…"

He'd strung five cranberries on the string and looked quite proud of himself. "What I mean is they weren't the kind of parents who baked pies, sang me to sleep or tried to give me advice about girls. But I didn't mind that—I'd had enough of people trying to make me into something I didn't want to be. These people were teachers, question askers, and they made me think. They inspired me to work my ass off. They were the reason I ended up going to Harvard."

Interesting, Olivia thought. It explained so much

about him. Why his whole life was his work—and why he'd do anything to protect it. "Did they end up adopting you?"

He shrugged. "In their way. I lived with them until I was twenty-one."

"Are they still around?"

He shook his head. "She died a year after he died."

"I'm sorry," she said softly. "It must be hard to be alone."

He stabbed another red cranberry, then glanced up at her through his thick lashes. "I'm not alone right now."

She'd never met a man like this one, never been so affected by anyone. In a matter of a few minutes he had her feeling sad, frustrated, unsure, angry, protective and now, aroused. "Does growing up the way you did make you want kids, or not?"

There was no flash of revulsion or even dislike for the idea in his gaze, only a look of frank sincerity. "I can't imagine being able to love anyone that much. I don't think I'm capable of it—you need to see love from a very early age to be able to learn how to give it."

It surprised her that he'd given the idea so much thought. "It helps, probably, but I don't think it's a necessity. I think love can be learned, just like history or reading."

"Or chemistry?" he offered, amusement dancing in his eyes.

She nodded. "Exactly." Then she leaned in and kissed him on the mouth. A soft kiss at first, coaxing him to open for her, taste her. And when he did, she sighed. He'd eaten some of the popcorn when she hadn't been looking because his lips were slightly and deliciously salty. "I'm not going to wait for you to finish your garland."

"Sweetheart," he uttered huskily, "I was about to throw the whole damn tree out the window."

The tip of his tongue ran across her lips in one silken stroke and she smiled, touched his face with one hand. He had the slight scratch of a day's worth of beard, and the rough feeling acted like a drug on her. She angled her head and kissed him hard, reveling in the wounded, turned-on sound he made as he returned her kiss, then nipped at her bottom lip.

"I've come prepared tonight, Ms. Winston," he said, his eyes blazing with hunger.

"I hope you've come doubly, maybe even triply, prepared."

A hoarse chuckle escaped his throat. "I'm glad we're on the same page because there's no way I'm letting you out of my bed before sunup."

He was just about to kiss her again when there was a soft knock at the door. Mac cursed brutally. "I might have to kill the person on the other side of that door."

He pushed to his feet, stalked to the door and flung it wide. Johnny. He looked embarrassed.

"I'm sorry to bother you, sir," he said, then caught sight of Olivia. "And you, Miss Winston—but Mr. DeBold needs to speak with Mr. Valentine immediately."

When Mac first arrived and saw Harold DeBold sitting on the couch in his living room having a beer, he wasn't sure what the man wanted to see him about. Maybe he was freaked out about becoming a dad and wanted to talk about it, or about Louise. Or maybe he wanted their financial plans to change immediately to include the child.

Then Mac noticed another beer on the coffee table, opened, sweat beading on the bottle, and for the first time since he'd met the DeBolds his confidence in having them as clients waned.

Harold gestured for Mac to sit. "I apologize for interrupting your evening."

Mac wasn't up for pleasantries—not tonight. "What's this about?"

"I didn't know Olivia's father was Owen Winston."

Mac frowned.

"He's a legend in the financial world," Harold continued.

Mac didn't like where this was going. He stared at Harold steadily. "Is there a point to this?"

Sensing Mac's irritation, Harold pointed to the bottle on the coffee table. "How about a drink? It's a great little microbrew from—"

"Harold," Mac interrupted tightly, "with all due respect, I don't want a goddamn thing except to know where you're going with this Owen Winston thing."

Harold grinned at that, then nodded. "I just got off the phone with him, Mac."

"You called him?"

"No. He called me."

"Looking for his daughter?"

"He wanted to warn me about you." Harold took a heavy swallow of beer. "But he also doesn't like that you're here with his daughter, that's for sure."

Mac grabbed the bottle of beer from the table and drained it. Then he stood. "Thank you for your time, Harold."

"You know, it was ballsy of you to hire her."

Mac shrugged. "It was calculated."

"Okay, then it was ballsy of her to take the job."

Ballsy…? Maybe the better word was unethical. Strange. Olivia had called him immoral once, but he'd never broken his client's trust—not like she just had. "I assume we're done here?"

"Of course. I don't want to keep you. But, Mac…" Harold stood, regarded him seriously. "I don't believe in rumors or the pissed-off ramblings of a jealous rival. I go on what I see. You have our business." He shrugged. "I just thought you should know."

Mac should have been thrilled—or hell, satisfied—but all he felt was the urge to shove his fist through a wall.

"Thank you, Harold." Mac shook his hand, then walked out of the room and out of the house.

Outside, the bitter wind slammed him in the face, small bits of snow pelting him from all sides. But he hardly felt it. From day one, he had been out to screw Olivia Winston, both physically and emotionally, and had ended up being screwed himself.

He spied her cottage, the lights of the Christmas tree inside glowing through the large bay window. She was a sly one, he had to give her that. But her little betrayal was going to pale in comparison with what he had planned for her next.

Seventeen

Olivia had little practice at seduction. She'd never been to a Victoria's Secret store or trolled the bookstores looking for the most recent printing of *How to Please a Man*. Instead, she was relying on the good old-fashioned art of being naked on a bed to get Mac right where she wanted him. And that would be on top of her…

On the other side of the room, the fire blazed in the hearth, warming the room and subsequently her skin. She was a little nervous. This was major exposure, total vulnerability, every flaw out there to be judged and inspected. For a moment, she contemplated greeting Mac from under the covers, but decided against it.

The door opened and Mac walked in, bringing a blast of frigid air with him. He was back so soon. Must've been nothing all that important with Harold, she thought, just guy talk. She shifted on the bed so she was lying sideways like one of those women in a Botticelli painting. Then he looked up and saw her. When he realized that she was nude, a flush of heat rolled up his neck. In one easy movement, he closed the door, then went to the edge of the bed.

Olivia's heart beat strongly in her chest. "Everything good?"

He nodded, his eyes dark and intense as he stared down at her. "Perfect." He unbuttoned his shirt and removed his pants. "Exactly what I was hoping for."

Anxious excitement played in Olivia's belly as Mac crawled toward her like an animal at feeding time. When he had her in his arms, he paused for a moment and just looked at her, her skin, her breasts. Then he leaned forward and took one soft peak into his mouth.

Olivia sucked air between her teeth and melted back onto the bed. This was what she'd wanted, what she'd hoped for tonight. She couldn't wait to have him inside of her. She closed her eyes and reveled in the feel of Mac on top of her. His skin, the way his muscles flexed and hardened as he moved down her body, planting kisses on her ribs, then her belly.

As he moved downward, Olivia smiled. She knew where he was going and she reached for his hair, fisted his scalp. His head dropped between her thighs. She felt his hands between her legs, pressing them apart, his fingers raking up her skin, opening the hot, wet folds. Her rational mind fell apart, and all that was left in her brain was the place that registered pleasure. And then he was licking her, soft, quick laps that had her legs trembling with excitement. Her fingers gripped his hair as he continued suckling her, as she bucked against his mouth. She could barely hold on. The feeling was too strong, too intense.

"Oh, Mac…I'm going to…"

He must've heard the desperation in her voice, knew she was on the brink of climax, because he lifted off of her, grabbed the foil packet that had been in his jeans and sheathed himself.

He entered her with one hard thrust. Olivia cried out, her body wracked with heat and energy as she took him fully. He slipped his hands under her hips and squeezed her closer, then pulled out and slammed back into her again. Olivia felt the initial thunder of climax coming over her and her body reacted. She bucked under him, her hands searching for his chest, her nails digging into the flesh over his muscle.

He bent his head, covered her mouth with his in a deep, all-consuming kiss. Olivia started to whimper, the core of her shaking and pulsing until her body could no longer contain the hot, decadent energy inside and she erupted. Her head dropped to one side, then the other as she cried out in several painful-sounding screams that seemed to rip right through Mac.

He pounded into her, over and over, until she thought he might rip her apart. But when she straightened her legs and spread them wide, he stiffened, groaned and thrust deeply inside of her, bucking, pounding, until he gave in and took his own release.

In the moments afterward, Mac stayed on top of her, his hips flexing and shuddering with the aftermath of release. But as soon as her arms went around his neck and threaded into his hair, Mac pulled himself away and off the bed.

Olivia stared after him, her body still achy and warm from his touch. "What's wrong?"

He sat there, his back to her. Then from deep in his chest, he started laughing. It was not a pleasant, happy sound, but dark and ominous.

"What?" Olivia asked softly.

Mac glanced over his shoulder, his gaze eerily satisfied. "I had no idea you were as ruthless as me."

A waft of cold air moved through her. "What are you talking about?"

"I have to say I'm impressed."

"Impressed with what?" He didn't look like himself. He was dark and sad, and Olivia suddenly felt very naked. Covering herself with a throw, Olivia asked, "What is wrong with you?"

"During my drink with Harold he informed me that he had just gotten off the phone with your father."

Olivia's heart sank. "No...."

"To warn him about me."

Olivia swallowed hard.

Mac stood and threw his shirt on. "I wonder how he knew I was with the DeBolds."

This was not happening, Olivia thought with deep

frustration and disappointment. How could she have made such a mistake? How could her father be such an ass? "I'm sorry. I told him where I was going, but—"

"And that I was going, too, right?"

"Yes, but—"

"I remember you calling me immoral…."

"Mac, I know you're angry and I get why. And I don't blame you. But if you look at the situation for what it is, I did nothing wrong here."

He put his pants on. "Really. How do you figure that?"

She came up on her knees, the throw pressed to her chest. "We're not working together on this trip. Our job ended when I left your house. I'm working for Louise, and I had every right to tell my father where I was."

"Where you are, yes. Not where I am." He put on his coat. "Good thing Harold and Louise don't believe lies spread by tired, envious, unscrupulous old men."

"Stop that." She hated what he was saying because now she was starting to believe it was true.

Dressed and ready to walk out, Mac paused and looked at her. His gaze was filled with disrespect. "I believe we're even, don't you?"

"*We're* even?" she repeated. "Who are you referring to, Mac? Me and you? Or you and my father."

His lips thinned dangerously, then he shrugged as if he couldn't care less. "Take your pick."

"Well, you did nothing to me," she said tightly. "I'm not hurt or humiliated. You wanted me and I wanted you. I'm done obsessing about my past, about mistakes I've made. I enjoyed every moment of us."

For one second—just a split second—his eyes softened. Then the walls closed once again and he uttered a terse, "Well, perhaps that's where the revenge lies then. There's no more *us* to enjoy."

He closed the door behind him, and Olivia just stared after him. An hour ago, that door had been the heaven's gate her lover had walked through. Now, it represented the enormous barrier between them.

She dropped back onto the bed. She had told him the truth. She felt no shame in the choices that she'd made. She had wanted Mac as much as he had wanted her, and though they were never going to be together this way again, she had no regrets for making love to him one last time.

Because, no matter how much he despised her now, she felt sure of one thing—that's what it had been for her.

Love.

Eighteen

Morning-afters were usually filled with headaches or heartaches. Olivia's was filled with both. She had struggled to get through the two-hour breakfast lesson with Louise, overcooking the hollandaise, then dropping the pan to the floor when the woman had mentioned that Mac had indeed left late last night—on his own plane, of course.

If she were a more carefree woman, Olivia mused, stepping out of the DeBolds' limousine and gathering up her bags, she'd just chock the whole thing up to a great fling, and the reason she had finally let go of her shame about the past. Mac had made her feel good—nothing wrong with that. She was an adult now, and she deserved pleasure, even if the man giving it would never love her back.

"Have a safe flight, Olivia," Louise said, waving from the window of the limousine.

Olivia shouldered her bag, then waved back. "Thanks for everything."

"No—thank you. I'll let you know what happens on Thanksgiving."

Her evil smile made Olivia laugh. "Give 'em, hell, Louise."

The woman smiled and waved again, then rolled up the window and the car pulled away. Olivia walked toward the plane and boarded. As she sat in her leather bucket seat waiting for takeoff, she thought about herself and Mac and their backgrounds, and how their pasts had totally dictated their present. He'd been abandoned, and had learned to survive in the only way he could. And he had survived—he'd gone to the top of his profession. She'd been abandoned, too, but unlike him, she hadn't fought—instead, she'd refused to deal with her pain and had looked for help in the wrong place.

So she understood his anger, and the fear behind it.

She fell asleep thinking about him, and woke up in Minneapolis with a neck cramp and a small twinge of hope that maybe she'd see him again. She got her car from long-term parking and drove home. For the first time in a long time, her apartment felt warm and safe, and for the rest of the night, she ignored the blinking light on her answering machine and settled under her comforter to watch *Bridget Jones's Diary*.

Tomorrow was a huge day. She had menus to execute

and staff to boss around. Ethan and Mary's holiday engagement ball had been in the works for weeks, but it was the last thing Olivia wanted to think about. Celebrating her friend's happiness was a must-do, of course, and she'd never shirk her duty, but because of who Ethan was, the event was going to be a blowout. The whole of Minneapolis was going to be there, and she couldn't help wondering if maybe that meant a certain financial genius was going to show up....

Olivia pulled the covers up to her chin, aimed the remote at the TV and pushed Play.

Ah...Colin Firth.

Mac's lungs were about to explode, and his legs felt shaky, but he didn't stop running.

It was coming up on 5:00 a.m. and he'd been in the gym of his office building on the treadmill for over an hour, trying to get his brain to shut down. Unfortunately, it looked as though his body was going to go first.

He stabbed the off button on the machine and reached for his towel. Damn it, he thought, walking unsteadily to his private locker room. When he'd left Door County two days ago, he'd counted on the fact that he wouldn't have to see Olivia Winston for months.

It wouldn't be nearly that long.

Mac hated tuxedos about as much as he hated over-the-top parties, but he was a slave to business, and after learning that one of his former clients was going to be at Ethan Curtis's engagement party tonight, he'd reconsidered the invite. Ethan Curtis was marrying Mary

Kelley, Olivia's business partner, so she was definitely going to be there.

He'd broken things off with many women in his time, and had never given a second thought to seeing them again. It was just this woman—she made him feel like a weak animal, a constantly hungry animal. He had to get her out of his system.

He stripped and headed for the shower. Maybe the best way to get Olivia out of his head was to force himself to see her again, be reminded of her betrayal. Or maybe he was just kidding himself and tonight was going to be just as hellish as the past two nights had been.

The top floor of the world-famous building rotated at the pace of one revolution per hour—that way the guests who were partaking in food and drink wouldn't get dizzy and lose their lunches in the first five minutes.

A wise plan by the architect, Olivia mused as she left the kitchen after inspecting each and every serving platter before it went out. She spotted Mary talking to Tess by the window and headed their way. Her blond hair piled on top of her head, Mary was wearing an off-the-shoulder gray silk dress, her protruding belly stretching the material in a lovely, earthy way. And looking especially glamorous in a brick-red minidress and matching heels, her red hair loose and blown straight, was Tess. Olivia watched as No Ring Required's resident hard-ass reached out and touched Mary's stomach, her smoky eyes shining with warmth.

"Well, well, well," Mary said when Olivia approached, her gaze running over Olivia's strapless chocolate-brown pencil dress. "Can I say it again, Miss Winston? You look hot."

Tess snorted. "That word should not be coming out of a pregnant woman's mouth."

Laughing, Mary remarked, "How do you think I got this way in the first place?"

Pretending to cover her ears, Tess said, "Okay, too much information."

Feeling self-conscious for a moment, Olivia smoothed the fabric of her skirt and glanced around at the party, which was packed and in full swing. She'd dressed carefully for Mary's engagement party. After all, she was wearing two hats—guest and worker—so she had needed to find the right combo. And then there was the not insignificant fact that Mac might be coming. She wasn't going to lie to herself and pretend that seeing him hadn't affected her choice in wardrobe.

"Did you see your father yet?" Tess asked, pulling her from her thoughts.

Olivia shook her head. "Where is he?"

"Over at the bar."

Olivia had been trying to get hold of her father for the past two days, but he'd been in Boston on business and hadn't returned her calls.

"So," Mary said cozily, "before Ethan steals me away, are you going to tell us how Door County went?"

"No."

Tess lifted a brow at Olivia's succinct reply. "Uh-oh."

"Was I right?" Mary asked gently. "About going out

of town together? Did you two…hmm, how to put this delicately…"

"Forget delicately," Tess interrupted. "Did you get busy with the guy?"

Olivia felt red all over. "C'mon, Tess. Jeez."

Tess gave Mary a look. "That's a yes."

"Tess," Mary said, warning in her gaze, "I hope you've learned from this—never go out of town with a guy you find attractive."

"Please…he'd have to slip something in my double espresso and carry me off for that to happen, and God help him if he did that." Tess was looking around the room as she spoke, and in a matter of seconds her whole demeanor changed. Her skin went white as milk and she stared, fixated on something.

Both Mary and Olivia saw the change and turned to see what was affecting Tess in such a way, but in the sea of people, they couldn't tell who or what was the cause.

"What's wrong, Tess?" Olivia asked.

"I swear I just saw…someone I knew a long time ago."

"Old boyfriend?"

"I suppose you could call him that. He looks so different—it can't be him."

Mary attempted to lighten the mood. "Did he look better or worse?"

"He looked bored and aloof, and utterly gorgeous." She kept searching the crowd. "It can't be him." She turned back to them, color returning to her cheeks. "Seeing people from the past is an awkward thing."

It was all she said, but Olivia knew it had to be more

than feeling awkward. Tess had actually looked panic-stricken. But Olivia didn't get to inquire further because at that moment Ethan walked over to them and slipped his arm around Mary's growing waist. "Can I take my girl? There's a coat check up front calling our name."

Mary rolled her eyes. "You are such an exhibition-ist, Ethan."

"It's one of the reasons you love me, right?"

She smiled at Olivia and Tess, then kissed her soon-to-be husband. "Of course, honey."

When they'd walked away, indeed toward the coat check, Tess quickly excused herself, too, saying that she was going to see about something.

Then, Olivia spotted her father speaking to two men by the bar and she headed his way.

Standing near the jazz band, Mac watched Olivia dance with her father. She looked beautiful tonight, and even though he'd tried to put her out of his mind, his body remembered everything. Clearly, it was going to take a helluva lot of time and effort to forget her.

She caught his eye then, and blanched. She hadn't expected him, and she looked both hopeful and worried. His hands itched to touch her, kiss her. If he had any pride, any sense, he'd walk away from the situation and never look back. But he was an idiot.

Pushing away from the stage, he walked toward her just as the song was ending.

Owen spotted him, too, and gritted his teeth as Mac walked up. "What are you doing here?"

"Retrieving an old client," Mac said easily.

"Oh, yes, I saw you talking with Martin Pollack. I suppose he's willing to overlook your—"

"Stop, Owen. This story of yours is growing so old there's mold on it. Everyone knows you lied, they're just waiting for you to admit it."

"I'm not admitting anything."

"Suit yourself. I don't give a damn anymore." He looked at Olivia. "You look beautiful tonight."

"Thank you." Her eyes glittered with warmth, and something else…something he couldn't quite name.

"Are you having a good time?"

"Not really."

Owen stared at her. "Let's go, Olivia."

But Olivia wouldn't take her eyes off of Mac. "It's okay."

Mac was confused. "What is?"

"If you need to do it, I understand. You have me and my father here."

"What are you talking about?"

She smiled, a little sadly. "The great revenge. What it's all been for."

"Oh, Liv…" Mac shook his head. She didn't get it. She thought when he'd walked out the other night he was still bent on payback. She didn't understand that what she'd done had pissed him off as a man—not a businessman.

"What did you do to my daughter?" Owen said menacingly.

"Dad, that's enough," Olivia said.

But Owen wasn't listening. "If you hurt her—"

"I'm serious, Dad. You've caused enough trouble." Olivia glared at her father. "One more word about Mac, and our relationship will be irrevocably damaged. Do you understand me?"

Owen looked shocked. "Olivia."

A surge of need moved through Mac. It was so powerful it took him completely by surprise, and he reached for Olivia's hand and lifted it to his mouth. After he kissed the palm, he spoke to Owen, but he looked into Olivia's chocolate eyes. "You have an amazing daughter, Winston. Beautiful and brilliant. I tried like hell to make her pay for your mistakes, but she'd have nothing to do with me."

Owen said nothing.

Mac released Olivia's hand. Revenge was a useless thing. He was done. He nodded at Olivia, said good-night and walked away.

Nineteen

The party wasn't supposed to end until midnight, but Olivia just couldn't stay any longer. She asked Tess to cover for her, then grabbed her coat and headed for the elevator. Just as the doors were about to close, her father slipped inside.

"Dad, I said good night to you…." She knew she sounded peevish, but she didn't care. She wanted one thing right now and any interruptions were unwelcome ones.

"Sweetheart, I just had to tell you that I'm so proud of you."

"For what?" she asked impatiently.

"Keeping that snake away from you."

That was it. Olivia reached out and pulled the emergency stop button. The elevator came to a jolting stop, and her father looked at her like she was crazy.

"What's going on?"

"I love you, Dad, but I'm not doing this any longer. Get this straight, I'm not Grace—"

"What?"

"I'm not your sister. I'm not Grace. Her life is not mine." She looked at him, her gaze serious. "What I am is a grown woman who is not going to cater to her father's fears about a life he can't control."

Owen's neck reddened. "Olivia..."

"My personal life is my own. Period." Owen looked very stuffy in his tuxedo, very impervious, but she went on. "Now, about Mac. You're going to leave him alone. Bottom line is, I love the guy, and if we can both get past how we met and why we were brought together, I think there might be a future in it for us."

Her father looked horrified. "No...."

She took a breath and softened at the look of despair on his face. "What do you have against him, other than the fact that he wanted to punish you for lying to his clients?"

For a second, Owen looked as though he was going to deny it, then he dropped his gaze and stared at his shoes. "Getting old isn't graceful or easy. People treat you like you might break, like you can't take the heat— they think your mind isn't what it used to be."

Olivia touched his arm. She loved her father—even with all his faults, and there were many. She rolled up on her toes and kissed him on the cheek. "Do the right thing, Dad. You're a great money man, a legend—everyone thinks so. Just be that for as long as you can." She reached out and flipped down the emergency stop button. The elevator descended. "The truth will come out eventually. Don't make this foolish mistake be your legacy. Take care of it."

Owen was silent for a moment, then he nodded.

The doors opened to the lobby and Olivia stepped out. "I have somewhere I need to be. Good night, Dad."

He gave her a tight smile and uttered a soft, "Good night, Olivia," before the elevator doors closed again.

When Mac walked into his house an hour later, he felt like he didn't belong there. Every piece of furniture, every color on the walls, had been picked out by her. Why was it then that she herself wasn't here? Olivia belonged here, she belonged to him.

"Damn it," he muttered, going down the hall to his room. He was going to take a shower, then head over to Olivia's apartment. He was so tired of fighting for the stupid, inconsequential things in his life. He was going to fight for something real now. He was going to make her talk to him.

"I'm trying this again."

Instinctively, Mac prepared himself for a fight. Then the voice registered in his brain and he let it fall to the side as he looked up. There on his bed, lying back against his pillow, was Olivia. She was fully dressed, her dark hair tousled and loose, and she had a worried smile on her lips.

Mac stared at her. "How did you get in here?"

She held his gaze steady with hers. "I still have the key. You forgot to ask for it back."

He shook his head slowly. "I didn't forget."

The expression in her eyes turned hopeful and she said, "Mac, about tonight…and the DeBolds…"

He cut her off. "No."

But she was insistent. "Yes. I need to say this to you again." She pushed off the bed and walked over to him, stood before him. "I didn't think. I shouldn't have said a word about where I was. It was bad business, and I've learned from it. You could've lost the DeBolds—"

"Stop." He grabbed her arms and pulled her against him. "I don't give a damn about the DeBolds. Hell, I could've lost you." His gaze moved over her face. "From the very beginning, I put you in an impossible situation. I was a first-rate ass."

She bit her lip and her eyes misted over. "I have to tell you something. I talked with my father, and—"

"Sweetheart, I don't care," he said, truly meaning it. He'd never believed he was capable of the feelings he was having, the intensity of his feelings for her. "I don't care about any of that anymore. The only thing that matters to me is you, making you happy, making you smile, having you in my bed every morning. I'm tired of fighting, of doing battle." He reached out, brushed his fingertips across her cheek. "The only thing I'm going to fight for now is you…us."

Olivia could hardly believe what she was hearing. This was not the impenetrable tycoon she'd known when she had signed on to be his wife-for-hire. This was the loving, forgiving, generous man she'd hoped and prayed would walk into the room tonight and smile at her, accept her apology and go forward with her.

"Ever since I laid eyes on you, my life means something, Liv," he continued, taking her face in his hands. "Screw the money and the need for more, and more power to go with it. This is something good. You and me. I don't know what to do with it, but I know one thing, I'm not letting you go."

"Oh, Mac…"

He leaned in, kissed her on the mouth, a possessive, branding kiss that had her catching her breath. "I love you, Liv. I love you so much I ache."

"I love you, too." She laughed, pressed her forehead against his. "God, we're such idiots. Our intentions going into this thing were so stupid."

"True, but if they hadn't been we never would have found each other."

She nodded. "Or the way out of the past."

"Damn right." He kissed her again, a deep kiss that had her melting into him. Groaning with need, he murmured against her mouth, "Sweetheart, stay with me, love me. I want you to be mine forever."

Olivia smiled, her heart so full and happy. "Yes." She couldn't believe she was hearing him say that he loved her—it was a miracle.

Mac looked up then, his eyes burning with desire. "I'm going to marry you."

Olivia tried to fight back the tears, but it was useless. She nodded, and choked out, "Okay."

He brushed away the tear from her cheek. "Make babies with you."

"Yes. Yes." She threw her arms around his neck and held on tight. From a shameful past that had held her hostage for so long, to a light, loving future with the man of her dreams. How was it possible? She was so lucky.

Mac took her mouth in a slow, pulse-pounding kiss. "I love you, Mrs. Valentine."

"Sounds strange, doesn't it?" she whispered against his mouth, feeling so vulnerable, yet so loved.

He shook his head and nibbled at her lower lip. "No way, sweetheart. Sounds just right."

* * * * *

Brad shoved the truck into gear and drove to the bottom of the hill, where the road forked. Turn left, and he'd be home in five minutes. Turn right, and he was headed for Indian Rock.

He had no damn business going to Indian Rock.

He had nothing to say to Meg McKettrick, and if he never set eyes on the woman again, it would be two weeks too soon.

He turned right.

He couldn't have said why.

He just drove straight to the Dixie Dog Drive-In.

Back in the day, he and Meg used to meet at the Dixie Dog, by tacit agreement, when either of them had been away. It had been some kind of universe thing, purely intuitive.

Passing familiar landmarks, Brad told himself he ought to turn around. The old days were gone. Things had ended badly between him and Meg anyhow, and she wasn't going to be at the Dixie Dog.

He kept driving.

He rounded a bend, and there was the Dixie Dog. Its big neon sign, a giant hot dog, was all lit up and going through its corny sequence—first it was covered in red squiggles of light, meant to suggest ketchup, and then yellow, for mustard.

Brad pulled into one of the slots next to a speaker, rolled down the truck window and ordered.

A girl roller-skated out with the order about five minutes later.

When she wheeled up to the driver's window, smiling, her eyes went wide with recognition, and she dropped the tray with a clatter.

Silently Brad swore. Damn if he hadn't forgotten he was a famous country singer.

The girl, a skinny thing wearing too much eye makeup, immediately started to cry. "I'm sorry!" she sobbed, squatting to gather up the mess.

"It's okay," Brad answered quietly, leaning to look down at her, catching a glimpse of her plastic name tag. "It's okay, Mandy. No harm done."

"I'll get you another dog and a shake right away, Mr. O'Ballivan!"

"Mandy?"

She stared up at him pitifully, sniffling. Thanks to the copious tears, most of the goop on her eyes had slid south. "Yes?"

"When you go back inside, could you not mention seeing me?"

"But you're Brad O'Ballivan!"

"Yeah," he answered, suppressing a sigh. "I know."

She rolled a little closer. "You wouldn't happen to have a picture you could autograph for me, would you?"

"Not with me," Brad answered.

"You could sign this napkin, though," Mandy said. "It's only got a little chocolate on the corner."

Brad took the paper napkin and her order pen, and scrawled his name. Handed both items back through the window.

She turned and whizzed back toward the side entrance to the Dixie Dog.

Brad waited, marveling that he hadn't considered incidents like this one before he'd decided to come back home. In retrospect, it seemed shortsighted, to say the least, but the truth was, he'd expected to be—Brad O'Ballivan.

Presently Mandy skated back out again, and this time she managed to hold on to the tray.

"I didn't tell a soul!" she whispered. "But Heather and Darlene *both* asked me why my mascara was all smeared." Efficiently she hooked the tray onto the bottom edge of the window.

Brad extended payment, but Mandy shook her head.

"The boss said it's on the house, since I dumped your first order on the ground."

He smiled. "Okay, then. Thanks."

Mandy retreated, and Brad was just reaching for the food when a bright red Blazer whipped into the space beside his. The driver's door sprang open, crashing into the metal speaker, and somebody got out in a hurry.

Something quickened inside Brad.

And in the next moment Meg McKettrick was standing practically on his running board, her blue eyes blazing.

Brad grinned. "I guess you're not over me after all," he said.

Silhouette

SPECIAL EDITION™

**brings you a heartwarming
new McKettrick's story from**

NEW YORK TIMES BESTSELLING AUTHOR

LINDA LAEL MILLER

THE
McKETTRICK
Way

Meg McKettrick is surprised to be reunited
with her high school flame, Brad O'Ballivan,
who has returned home to his family's
neighboring ranch. After seeing Meg again,
Brad realizes he still loves her. But the pride
of both manage to interfere with love...until
an unexpected matchmaker gets involved.

— McKettrick Women —

Available December wherever you buy books.

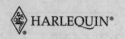

HARLEQUIN®

American ★ Romance®

Kate Merrill had grown up convinced
that the most attractive men were incapable
of ever settling down. Yet the harder she
resisted the superstar photographer
Tyler Nichols, the more persistent the
handsome world traveler became.
So by the time Christmas arrived, there
was only one wish on her holiday list—
that she was wrong!

LOOK FOR

THE CHRISTMAS DATE

BY

Michele Dunaway

**Available December
wherever you buy books**

ATHENA FORCE

Heart-pounding romance and thrilling adventure.

She's their ace in the hole.

Posing as a glamorous high roller, Bethany James, a professional gambler and sometimes government agent, uncovers a mob boss's deadly secrets…and the ugly sins from his past. But when a daredevil with a tantalizing drawl calls her bluff, the stakes—and her heart rate—become much, much higher. Beth can't help but wonder: Have the cards been finally stacked against her?

ATHENA FORCE

Will the women of Athena unravel Arachne's powerful web of blackmail and death…or succumb to their enemies' deadly secrets?

Look for

STACKED DECK
by *Terry Watkins.*

Available December wherever you buy books.

REQUEST YOUR FREE BOOKS!

2 FREE NOVELS PLUS 2 FREE GIFTS!

Silhouette Desire

Passionate, Powerful, Provocative!

YES! Please send me 2 FREE Silhouette Desire® novels and my 2 FREE gifts. After receiving them, if I don't wish to receive any more books, I can return the shipping statement marked "cancel." If I don't cancel, I will receive 6 brand-new novels every month and be billed just $3.80 per book in the U.S., or $4.47 per book in Canada, plus 25¢ shipping and handling per book and applicable taxes, if any*. That's a savings of almost 15% off the cover price! I understand that accepting the 2 free books and gifts places me under no obligation to buy anything. I can always return a shipment and cancel at any time. Even if I never buy another book from Silhouette, the two free books and gifts are mine to keep forever.

225 SDN EEXJ   326 SDN EEXU

Name	(PLEASE PRINT)	
Address		Apt.
City	State/Prov.	Zip/Postal Code

Signature (if under 18, a parent or guardian must sign)

Mail to the **Silhouette Reader Service™**:
IN U.S.A.: P.O. Box 1867, Buffalo, NY 14240-1867
IN CANADA: P.O. Box 609, Fort Erie, Ontario L2A 5X3

Not valid to current Silhouette Desire subscribers.

Want to try two free books from another line?
Call 1-800-873-8635 or visit www.morefreebooks.com.

* Terms and prices subject to change without notice. NY residents add applicable sales tax. Canadian residents will be charged applicable provincial taxes and GST. This offer is limited to one order per household. All orders subject to approval. Credit or debit balances in a customer's account(s) may be offset by any other outstanding balance owed by or to the customer. Please allow 4 to 6 weeks for delivery.

Your Privacy: Silhouette is committed to protecting your privacy. Our Privacy Policy is available online at www.eHarlequin.com or upon request from the Reader Service. From time to time we make our lists of customers available to reputable firms who may have a product or service of interest to you. If you would prefer we not share your name and address, please check here. ☐

SDES07

Inside ROMANCE

Stay up-to-date on all your
romance reading news!

Inside Romance is a FREE quarterly newsletter
highlighting our upcoming series releases
and promotions.

Visit
www.eHarlequin.com/InsideRomance
to sign up to receive our complimentary newsletter today!

IRNL107